THE
FEAR

THE
FEAR

SPENCER HAMILTON

Nerdy**Wordsmith**

Copyright © 2020 by Spencer Borup

Published by Nerdy Wordsmith
www.spencerhamiltonbooks.com
www.nerdywordsmith.com

Edited by Amy Teegan
(www.amyteegan.com/editing)

Cover design by Milan Jovanovic
(www.99designs.com/profiles/chameleonstudio74)

Formatting by Sandeep Likhar
(www.likharpublishing.com)

Illustration by Nick Harper
(www.nickharperbooks.com)

First Edition, August 2020

ISBN 978-1-952075-03-2 (paperback)
ISBN 978-1-952075-02-5 (ebook)
ISBN 978-1-952075-04-9 (audiobook)

To my quarantine partner

AUTHOR'S NOTE

This is a work of fiction, and its characters and events are the product of the author's imagination. In its creation, the author has drawn inspiration from his own self-quarantine experience through the events of COVID-19. All epigraphs are satire and are used fictitiously.

THE
FEAR

I

FEAR

1

JACQUELINE & ASHLEY

"Listen, this Chinese disease— Listen to me, because I know more about this stuff than anybody, people always tell me I'm the smartest when it comes to this . . . whatever—maybe the smartest person alive, some say— Listen, this Dem hoax is fake news. It'll disappear before April, believe me. You have nothing to be afraid of."

—President Donald J. Trump
press briefing, March 12, 2020

THE FEAR BEGAN for Ashley on the same day as everyone else—on Friday the 13th, of all days.

But for Jacqueline the fear was impossible to trace back to any singular event and say, "There it is, that's the moment I began to lose hope." When does one begin to suspect something alien lurks just beneath the skin? Is it when the rest of the world alienates you, when you're taught from a very young age that people like you are monsters destined to burn in the fires of Hell for eternity?

Or is it more simple than that . . . when something appears right at your front door?

At your front door knocking.

If it was the latter, then Jacqueline remembered *that* moment. Or rather, the series of moments, set up like dominoes, or like a fuse, steadily sparking toward the dynamite strapped to her throbbing brain.

It was the end of the previous summer, the first of the sparks. She and Ash had finally went off as a married couple, had finally moved out of her parents' Podunk hometown—no more living under their shadow, no more domestic violence, something she and Ash had shared in their childhood homes. But were they really so naïve (the answer was yes, yes they were) to believe that Austin, the weird liberal bubble in Texas, would be any different? Hateful people stalked everywhere, in every habitat, like demons with skin masks to hide the telltale signs of the nightmare beneath. But back in August, all those months ago, before time moved like a slug—or a reanimated corpse, in fits and bursts—when they wore their own masks of naïveté, Jack and Ash strolled hand-in-hand to the river for a summer screening of the cinematic leviathan, *Jaws*.

They'd only just dropped in exhaustion, their last boxes pushed inside their new apartment, when Ash found the event on her phone. They'd been trying to find a way to fill the awkward silence, to cut the tension that had just descended over them like a shroud because of Jack's half-joking, half-serious comment. Jack had tapped one of the dozens of cardboard boxes with her foot, at the ASH MISC scrawled on the side, and said, "Oh good, I see you remembered to pack those journals you love more than me." It had been a hurtful thing to say, both of them knew, and it threatened to upset the electric excitement that still suffused the air, that charged feeling of having finally struck out on their own, in a new town, for their new life. Ash had found that distraction quickly, tonight on the city's calendar of events. She'd squealed, her usual enthusiasm bursting through her exhaustion and their brief bout of tension like it was an oil-shiny bubble.

"*Jack*, I've found our inaugural celebration!"

Jacqueline had been too bone-tired to do more than mumble, though she knew she'd probably catch Ash's contagion of effervescence soon enough. Ash was infectious.

"A screening of *Jaws* at the river! It's . . . ohmygod, like, a five-minute walk from here!"

"Babe," Jacqueline finally mustered, *pbbf*ing sweat from her lips. "I don't think I can even get up right now. No way we're walking."

Ash sat up. "No way we're *missing* this!" She scooted over the cool tile, sidling up to Jacqueline. Her long raven hair dangled over Jacqueline's face in wet strands, tickling her and forcing a laugh from her belly. "Come on, baby," Ash breathed, looming closer until Jack felt her breath on her eyelashes. "Don't you want to have an excuse to hold me when I'm scared? Someone has to protect me from the scary monster . . ."

Her lips brushed Jacqueline's, and they both closed their eyes. Ash's hair was a curtain, cutting them off from the rest of the world, their breath speeding and feeding into each other. Somehow Ash's sweat tasted sweeter on Jacqueline's tongue than her own. A heat flushed through her body, nothing like the exhaustion of their moving day.

Ash was contagious, all right.

After some time spent on that tile floor, the two women finally made the short walk to the river and found it infested with Austinites. Immediately they recognized that its reputation was deserved. Beneath the humid heat of a just-setting sun were all sorts: a man with a purple mohawk, a shirtless woman who couldn't have been younger than seventy years old, a kid on a unicycle, a gigantic Illustrated Man with a red-eyed Mastiff on a leash. This was exactly the crowd Jacqueline had hoped to see— people already walking on the far side of normal and thus less likely to sneer at two women holding hands.

Interspersed with the *Keep Austin Weird* crowd were the quintessential Texans, the ones Jacqueline had always pictured strutting around in ten-gallon MAGA hats and covetously clutching AK-47s. A part of her was still fearful of them, even in a city where she was supposed to be safe, and she shied away whenever they came near. She felt silly, though. What would Ash think?

The movie was great, as always—it was one of Ash's favorites, despite being released almost two decades before she was even born. And the crowd at the river absolutely loved it. There was a thrill that spread like a virus as soon as the movie opened with that group of young people partying at the beach. *That's just like us,* everyone's smiles said. And then the naked teenage girl. ("Boobs in a PG movie?!" Jack had exclaimed when Ash showed her the movie for the first time, feeling cheated that she hadn't seen *Jaws* growing up.) Then something hidden beneath the surface of the water latched on to the naked teenage girl and thrashed her around and around and she shrieked and screamed and cried out and bled out into the water and died; that scene sent a wave of cold delight around the riverside spectators. Jack felt it herself, that jolt on the nape of her neck. Whenever that iconic riff in the score cued up—

Dun dun . . . dun dun . . . dun dun dun dun dun-dun-dun-dun . . .

—Jack's heart would race, and she'd feel the fear on her skin. She swore that the bugs out here could taste that fear, were having a veritable feast from the breaker of fright rolling off of her and then crashing—

But then Ash would be there. Curled against her, laughing at her own fear and the crowd's reaction. The shark barely reared its head for most of the movie. That was Ash's favorite part, she always said, because everyone fears what they cannot see. But when it did, Ash squealed and buried her face against Jacqueline's damp skin, and Jack fell in love with her anew every time.

Maybe it was that effect the broken sharkbot had forced Spielberg to use and that ominous *dun-dun* of the iconic Williams score building up into a tangible dread, but all throughout the screening Jacqueline couldn't help but feel like she was being watched. She'd learned from experience that the glares of hate in Trump's grave new world were enough to sizzle on the skin. She could be looking at her phone in a café, totally unaware of her surroundings, and suddenly a prickle of pain would flash across her scalp. She'd look up and lock eyes with a corpulent neckbeard wearing a *Don't Tread On Me* shirt and sneering at her. Even if she didn't *look* queer, somehow they always routed her out.

And she had that feeling now—*Someone's watching me*—from *Jaws*'s opening shot to the rolling credits after those final lines of dialogue.

"I used to hate the water."

"I can't imagine why."

Ash chanted those last four words along with many others in the crowd, and suddenly Jacqueline felt silly—felt stupid—for letting such a ridiculous emotion ruin her entire evening. No one was watching her; Ash would have told her she was being paranoid. This was supposed to be their inaugural celebration of their new home. They now lived a short walk away from a river teeming with people who accepted them, who looked at them—Jacqueline, a curvy white bombshell, with her short, bubbly Asian-American wife clutching her—and smiled instead of jeered. Jack usually hated flaunting her body out in public, hated wearing bathing suits, had always felt exposed; she'd hoped it would be different here, away from California, but still, there it was again.

Someone's watching you, Jack . . .

Ash turned to her, radiating a glow of excitement. "I *love* that last line. It gets me every—damn—time!" She crowed out across the water, "I LOVE THIS MOVIE!" and someone shouted back "FUCK YEAH YOU DO, BITCH!" The whole crowd laughed and cheered. Ash turned back to Jacqueline, laughing as well, and Jack felt that familiar rush of guilt for not being in the moment, being present for her wife.

"I love you," she whispered to Ash, and just to prove that she wouldn't let her *someone's watching you* fear ruin the moment, she pulled Ash to her tippytoes and kissed her. Her wife beamed at her.

Nobody's watching me, she told herself, *except my wife.*

It took a while to wade through the throng of people

leaving the event. Luckily they didn't have to try to navigate their car through all this. Living so close to the excitement was definitely a perk that Jacqueline could get used to.

They'd barely extricated themselves from the heart of the crowd before Ash launched into an instant replay of all her favorite parts of the movie. But Jack didn't mind. She would ride the wave of her wife's infectious enthusiasm and let it wash the watched feeling from her skin.

"Wish that shark would eat you next, you dyke cunt."

The words were spoken so amiably that at first Jack and Ash didn't react. They kept walking, kept holding hands, but Ash stopped talking, and a fug of discomfort settled over them. It was as if someone in a waiting room had cut a loud fart, and though everyone braced themselves for the inevitable stink, no one was brave enough to acknowledge it.

"Maybe I'll do everyone a favor and throw you in the water myself."

The *someone's watching you* itch was back, crawling over her scalp. Jacqueline felt it cinch her skin tighter, suffocating her. "Ash . . ." she muttered, a moan rising from her gut.

"Just keep walking," Ash said calmly.

But to keep walking meant to leave the crowd of people. To isolate themselves. To possibly lead whoever was speaking directly to their front door.

"You hear me, bitch?"

Jacqueline's step faltered, but Ash dragged her along.

"Or that chink's muff suffocating you?"

Ash wheeled around. "*Fuck* you and stay the *fuck* away from us."

Jacqueline moaned again. Her body turned.

There, lit by the dying glow of the lights along the river they'd just left behind, was a hulking figure surrounded by a couple less-hulking, sniggering friends. Jack's eyes adjusted in the dim. The man yelling at them wasn't what she'd expected, and that somehow made it far worse, like some diseased misfiring byproduct of evolution had forgotten that dangerous bigots were supposed to *look* like dangerous bigots. Not like a social justice warrior wearing a cardigan and neatly shaped beard. Not with bright, intelligent eyes and a disarming countenance. This was the type of man Jacqueline could have fallen for, gone home and slept with, before she'd found Ashley; he even looked like one of her old high school boyfriends. Where was the MAGA hat? The bad complexion? The conspiracy theorist's crazed gleam?

"You gonna let this Jap speak for you, cunt?"

He was talking to her.

Say something.

But she was locked up. That fear, that fear she'd felt her whole life, had her gripped in a fist and wouldn't let go.

"This Jap is Chinese, dumbass." That was Ash, never afraid to face the monster. "Second generation, motherfucker. If you're going to use racial slurs, maybe take a moment to look at a map for once in your narrow-minded life."

His friends laughed, but the man's face colored. "Tell your bitch to watch her mouth before I watch it for her."

He was still talking to Jack.

And she still couldn't say anything back.

"Tell your bitch to go back to her own country."

Say something, Jack, say something . . .

"Then maybe I'll show you a good time." He grinned. "Cure you of your taste for cunt."

Jack couldn't breathe. It always came back to this—people thinking she was an imposter, that she didn't actually want to be with a woman, that she was lying to herself and they knew her better than she knew herself. The worst part was the inevitable moment when her mind betrayed her and she wondered if they were *right*.

Ash looked at her; it was a furtive glance before returning to the man ten feet away—you never look away from a rabid dog—but a glance that communicated so much.

Ash knew Jack's fear. Or rather, she knew *of* it. She didn't actually understand it. Ashley had always taken for granted the strong, bullheaded way she could stand against hate. She'd faced hate like this her whole life because the color of her skin wasn't something she could hide. But now she was asking the same of her wife, was saying with that glance: *Do something. Stand up for me. Don't do this again, Jack.*

That silent plea sent a spike of anger through Jack, piercing the freeze of fear. Anger at her wife for asking this of her. Anger at her wife for choosing Austin as their new home, for promising it would be different—

No. She wouldn't turn this on Ash. They were partners. She had meant every word of the vows she'd recited three summers ago on the best day of her life. She *still* meant them. Jacqueline and Ashley were a united front, a wall that no trickle or torrent could erode.

She turned her anger away from Ash and toward this stranger and his friends.

"You don't get to talk about my wife that way, asshole."

The man in the cardigan stepped closer, closing the gap of darkness between them. Shadows oozed down his face and pooled in the recesses of his grin. For the briefest of moments, Jack could have sworn that there was a burning, ethereal glint to his eyes; he seemed to her almost demonic.

"I'll do whatever the fuck I want, bitch. This is *my* country. Leave or be run out, faggot."

That last word, the *real* F word, shocked her into that glaze of fear again. She faltered, stuttering nonwords. The group of men laughed.

They're laughing at you, Jack, her mind told her.

Ash stepped forward. "Uh-uh. You don't get that word. That word's ours. Are *you* a faggot?"

The asshole and Jack both flinched at that. Jack *hated* when Ash used that word and she would always hate it no matter how many times Ash told her they had to "take back our word" and "use their fear against them, because that's what hate is, it's fear."

No, Ash, no, Jack thought.

"You—"

But the man didn't even bother finishing whatever he was going to say. He cut himself off, grunting with a burst of motion, cutting the space between them in half with one long-legged leap. Ash didn't react quick enough, and Jack saw that she was right in his path. He was going to trample her and their first night in Austin would be spent in the emergency room or maybe the morgue—

And for the second time in just as many minutes, Jack felt herself breaking from the fear and upholding her vows. She lurched out of her freeze. She grabbed Ash by her tiny shoulder and jerked her bodily behind her.

His fist hit Jack's left breast first, in a heavy *thud* that was probably meant for Ash's face but Jack's quick movement and height difference meant a punch to the boob, and *god* that *hurt*—

His second punch angled up and slammed into her bottom lip. Blood burst from her face, spraying his cardigan.

Ash, in her highest air-splitting falsetto, screamed.

His friends rushed forward, grabbing him, telling him they had to run and cops were coming and let the chink go. He resisted for a moment, grinning malevolently at Jack. The power of his gaze hit her in the gut like a third punch.

And then something inexplicable happened. A gauzy blackness rose from his shoulders, like giant, batlike wings. That glint came back to his eyes. And she knew. She knew he was the watchful demon. *Her* demon.

The moment lasted barely a second, and then he threw her down into the dirt and he let his friends drag him away, laughing.

Ash knelt over her, her raven hair once again a curtain cutting them off from the rest of the world. Jack could hear people running and calling to them—"Are you okay? Oh my god, did that guy attack you?"—and the humid Austin night boiled the blood from her skin and mixed it to a mud with the dirt. The dirt settled on her sweat-drenched body, and all she could hear was the droning of insects gorging themselves on her blood and on her fear, and all she could see was her wife's crying, beautiful face.

* * *

FOR ASHLEY, THE BEGINNING of the fear was much easier to trace.

It was the morning of March 13th—a Friday, the last day of the work week and the first day of her weekend, a time to celebrate, to party, to rush home with a bottle of wine and see if she could coax a smile from Jack's gorgeous face. Instead, she was staring at two screens.

The first was her phone, where she'd pulled up an urgent email from her company's CEO telling everyone to stay home indefinitely and that the sales team—the team Ashley headed—was terminated, effective immediately.

The second was the television, where CNN was streaming live footage of the President of the United States mandating a stay-at-home order because the deadly global pandemic had reached American soil.

2

ASHLEY

" 'The CDC is advising the use of . . . non-medical cloth face-covering as an additional voluntary public health measure—' So it's voluntary, you don't have to do it . . . I don't think I'm gonna be doing it."

—President Donald J. Trump
reading the White House announcement of
COVID-19 response CDC guidelines

THE SOUND OF THE TV fell away. Ashley's vision trebled, ghosts of the two screens merging and superimposing over each other—one announcing the loss of her job, the other the loss of . . . what? Her freedom? No, that was a bit too hyperbolic.

The loss of her future.

Yes, that sounded right. Still with a whiff of hyperbole, but maybe that was just an inevitable consequence of real life proving once and for all to be stranger than fiction.

She laughed at herself, then quickly shut her mouth— her teeth gave an audible *clink*, shocking her further out of her haze. Here she was laughing all alone in the living room. What would Jack think if she came in and saw her cackling like a loon at the President announcing a national shutdown?

Still, she couldn't help but laugh. All these thoughts, about the loss of freedoms and about her future looking like a dystopian wasteland, they were all so . . . *Jack*. This wasn't Ashley. Not Ash. She was always the one who took these things in stride, bounced back up into third gear and reassured her more contemplative wife that everything would be fine.

But the one-two punch of the loss of her job and of the world outside must have really shaken her. For the first time in a long while, her future wasn't laid out like a field before her, clear and planned and known. The mileposts had been ripped out.

She was more frightened of how Jack would take the news. If *Ash*, dependable, steady Ash, felt unmoored by this, how would her wife react?

Ashley stepped away from the TV, staring out the floor-to-ceiling window of their back wall. Jack had never been one to take change with any kind of grace. But ever since that night at the river, after *Jaws*, she'd become paranoid. Or more paranoid than usual.

Ashley felt guilty for thinking that, but it was true. That night, after picking her wife up off the ground and wiping the blood from her face, Ashley had found Jack inconsolable. She'd refused to say more than a few words to the police as they took her statement, sure that the authorities were somehow *in* on it, like they'd just let her assaulter saunter off with a high five and a wink.

Worse, she wouldn't go home. Ashley had to practically

drag her there—not an easy feat when you were five-foot-nothing and a solid thirty pounds lighter than your wife—and the whole time Jack squirmed with fear, sure that who she was now calling "the Cardigan Man" would jump out from a shadowy alley or was biding his time, following them to their new home so he could break in and skin Ash alive and rape Jacqueline.

Ashley shuddered. Their very first night in Austin and it had been an absolute nightmare. Jack had been feverish, blathering like a paranoid schizophrenic, so afraid to leave the safety of her own bed that she'd let her bladder loose sometime in the night. In all the commotion of trying to calm Jack down, they hadn't unpacked the bedding, so now there was a bright yellow stain in the center of the mattress.

A constant reminder of the Cardigan Man.

And the hysteria had only climbed to a fever pitch from there. It got so bad that, after three days of waking delirium, Jack announced that she had to get as far away from Austin as possible. Ashley of course couldn't do that—she started her new job in tech sales in only a week's time, and they had put all of their savings into moving halfway across the country.

But she had to do something. Unable to forcibly commit Jack (a thought that was admittedly only *half* joking), Ashley put her wife up in a hotel on the outskirts of the city for a few days and hoped Jack wouldn't do anything crazy while she was trying to figure out what they would do.

In the end, they did move. Not outside of Austin, but across the river and away from the city's bustling center. Sure, Ashley had to take out another line of credit, and they'd completely forfeited their deposit and paid a hefty fee to break the lease . . . and sure, this one-bedroom apartment was significantly smaller than their other place, and their new landlord was a lot to handle . . . but she was proud of what she had found as a solution.

But that had always been how their relationship worked—Jack needed support, and Ash needed to support. They worked well together in that way.

Their new apartment was a paranoid's dream: fairly close to downtown but not close at all, thanks to the winding, hilly roads to get there. Better yet, it was smack dab in the middle of a hoity-toity residential area full of pretentious yet quirky large homes fronted by gilded statue lions and mini wine vineyards. Apparently back in the '60s the residents had allowed architecture students from the local college to design and build an apartment complex in a little pocket where the curving backroads wound around a narrow river tributary. It seemed perfectly plausible to Ashley: the complex was old, unique, and would often burst into a surprising flare of what a student must have thought was "character," such as the pocked stones stacked to make the far connecting wall of their living room.

Take the window Ashley now looked through, for example. It was actually a huge double sliding door, even though they were on the second floor with no patio. It just opened into empty space. The landlord had removed the handle and screwed the sliding door in place after the previous tenant had drunkenly slid it open and stepped out . . . to a sobering drop to the cement patio below.

A stone's toss from where Ashley stood, a huge tree stretched up past their window. A big scarred, poorly trimmed Texas ash tree that crawled with chittering squirrels and held, impossibly, at the end of a long, quivering branch, a delicate hummingbird's nest. Past the tree was the creek, where some Austinites floated in kayaks—it seemed to Ash there was always someone out on that water—after which a slope dense with growth climbed far above, giving their eastward-facing wall the look of a living forest.

Below and to the right, a gated community pool was in view of their window. The deck was rotted in places, but with a view as verdant and paradisiacal as this, it was the perfect reading spot. The previous September when they'd first moved here, it was still quite warm, so Ashley had tried salvaging Jack's summer memories by enticing her to come out to swim. She'd even bought an inflatable pool float shaped like a gigantic diamond wedding ring. But now the thing floated dejectedly out on the water like a bloated corpse, slowly releasing its gasses into the surrounding atmosphere. Slowly poisoning paradise.

Like Jack's mind.

Ashley shook her head, scolding herself. She shouldn't be so harsh on Jack. Or she should at least be honest about it instead of hoarding these thoughts in her mind, behind her wife's back. But what kind of suspicions would breed from honesty such as this? If Jack couldn't even trust her partner . . .

Her brain would be a sac of spider eggs.

A bigger sac of spider eggs than it already was.

Again Ash scolded herself for thinking that way about Jack. Jack couldn't help it. She'd gone through a traumatic experience. She couldn't feel safe in this city, but she was trapped here because of the cost of getting here in the first place.

But hadn't Ashley gone through that same traumatic experience?

Hadn't the Cardigan Man said the worst things about *her*?

Hadn't *she* been the one stuck with finding them a new apartment, *she* the one who was scrambling to pay off their debt, *she* the one with the nine-to-five?

Well. No nine-to-five anymore.

What would they do now?

Ashley snapped herself out of it before she spiraled. This wasn't like her, to throw a pity party. The tactless way her boss's boss had just shit-canned her—*effective immediately*—had shocked her, that was all.

She scooped up the remote from the antique chest doubling as a coffee table and clicked off the television. God, making that horrible man stop his brainless bullshitting felt almost therapeutic.

Already feeling better, she bounded past the couch (and past the still-unopened bills on the floor), down the hall, and into their bedroom.

"Jack!"

No response. Ashley had stopped expecting responses. It was like a game: she really had to *earn* a reaction from Jack. Her wife had become a jack-in-the-box whose internal mechanism only sprung out for a horror-movie scare, when the audience isn't expecting it but is just begging to scream anyway.

"Guess who gets an early weeeeekennnnd?!"

And just as she'd hoped, she won the game and the jack-in-the-box sprang, muffled and somewhere amid the heap of bedding in the gloom:

"If the answer isn't 'Ash' then this is a horrible guessing game."

Ashley laughed and took a running leap at the bed. Entangling her limbs with the bedding-heap that was her wife, she tickled at random spots until she found Jack's tummy—the soft peach fuzz just beneath her belly button. She walked her fingers down the skin, teasing her wrist between Jack's thighs—

"Don't," Jack grunted, clamping her legs around Ashley's hand like a vise.

Ashley smiled, climbing on top of her. "Don't you want to play?"

"Started my period this morning."

In a flash, Ash's mind played another game: word association—or maybe Rorschach inkblots—and a smear of blood dripped from Jack's bottom lip and into the dirt, and it was the night of the Cardigan Man—

No, she told herself, shaking away the image like a spiderweb. *Be fun, Ash. Jack needs fun.*

But Jack wouldn't make fun easy, either. Ashley usually knew when Jack was on her period, and she didn't think that was today, though maybe it had started early. Or, more likely, Jack wasn't in the mood and this was her way of saying, *No touching.*

She disentangled herself from Jack, bounding across the bed and to the window—this one much smaller than the faux sliding door—and pulled the blinds up as far as they would go. Late morning sunlight streamed inside, banishing the shadows from the bedroom, illuminating heaps of laundry and old takeout containers and Jack's art supplies spread across her repurposed yoga mat. The place was a pigsty, but Ashley didn't mind letting Jack have her own little dark domain. She preferred the open, sunny main room when she was awake anyway.

Jack hissed at the sunlight, diving under the comforter.

Ashley laughed. "God, Jack, what are you, a vampire?"

Muffled voice: "If I were I'd drink my own blood and get it over with."

"Mmm, period blood? Too much iron. If you're gonna be a vampire, at least have some kind of *palate*. Personally, I'd drink John from downstairs. He seems like he'd have classy blood, easy to stomach. A nice Merlot."

Jack whipped the comforter off of herself. "John's *gay*, Ash."

Ashley laughed again. "Who said anything about *sex*? I thought you were on your period." She sat on the edge of the bed, throwing a pillow playfully at Jack. "You need to lay off the Anne Rice novels."

Pouting, Jack dove back down, burying her face in the pillow.

Ashley had to suppress a sigh. She personally loved the eclectic group of neighbors surrounding them. John, with his bodybuilder six-pack and opera rehearsals on his piano. Mo, on the other side of the stone wall, with his big beard and kind eyes and quiet manner, not talkative but always leaving little gifts for them—eggs from his daughter's chicken coop or a book on Austin history he thought they'd enjoy. Melanie just beneath them, who seemed to be perpetually hammering nails and apparently never ran out of wall space for picture frames. Edith a few doors down, who had lived here since 1969 and would probably die in that apartment. The group of women downstairs in the corner apartment—Ashley had heard they were actually a coven of witches. And all the outdoorsy types who kept canoes and kayaks down by the creek.

But Jack hated any mention of neighbors, because one of those outdoorsy types . . .

The Cardigan Man.

ASHLEY HADN'T BELIEVED HER when Jack first burst inside the apartment one evening in late September, just a few weeks after their second move. Jack had blasted through the front door screaming about how the Cardigan Man had found her, was here to murder her and molest her and rip her from Ash. Ash had convinced Jack to go down to the washers and dryers to switch a load of their clothes over to the next cycle. Maybe a little outside air would do her good, would put some color in her cheeks, might even convince her the outside world wasn't crawling with monsters that wanted to kill her. But instead her wife had come back looking even more manic, even more sallow. Her huge eyes were rolling in their sockets, saucers of glistening white.

"The Cardigan Man!" she screamed. *"He found us!"*

It took Ashley almost an hour to get the full story from her, and by then she just knew their clothes would be moldering in a heap in one of the silent machines. She had to go get them, probably run them through another cycle. Still in the front entry, where Jack had collapsed, she helped her wife up and scooped a few quarters from the ceramic bowl on the entryway table.

"No!" Jack gasped out. "You can't go—you can't—he'll—"

"Shhh, baby," Ash soothed. "I believe you. I believe

you saw him."

Jack blinked, grateful yet confused. "Then why——?"

"I've gotta get our laundry, baby," she said calmly. "Can't let the Cardigan Man steal our clothes, can I? I'll be quick, I promise."

"You . . ." A blankness fogged her gaze. "He's out there."

"I know, I believe you, I do! I'll take a key in case I need to gouge his eyes out. You know I can, too."

It was like talking to a child, but then, as much as Ashley loved her, Jack was often exactly that. Some important link in the chain of nurturing hadn't been provided to her—a common occurrence when ultra conservatives had an uneasy feeling their daughter might not be in to boys. Jack had entered adulthood with certain blind spots, or sometimes complete regressions like the one brought on by their night out to the river the month before.

With Jack placated as much as she'd allow, Ashley grabbed a key and stepped out, hearing their bolt slam into place the moment the door closed behind her. Seeing nobody along the walkway, she crossed to the stairs and skipped down.

The front of the complex wasn't nearly as idyllic as the creek side, with its gravel expanse haphazardly covered by cars always vying for room with no painted parking lines. But she did like how someone had taken the time to hang the bottom walkway with all sorts of vines and potted plants—and someone else had hidden a regiment of little plastic army men among those potted plants. She wanted to meet this neighbor; they seemed fun.

She reached a tunnel breezeway that connected the

parking lot side to the pool-and-creek side, with the second floor apartments bridging overhead. There across from the laundry room was a bulletin board where residents often left notes for each other or placed random items like used coffee makers that were up for grabs. That day, someone had pinned a sheaf of paper there. Ashley kept hoping to see some kind of potluck or invitation to the pool. That might be a way she could get Jack out of her room before she went completely agoraphobic.

On closer inspection, it looked like an anonymous resident had printed out a bunch of emails from their landlord. Ashley laughed. They hadn't yet been here one month and Doug had already bombed their inboxes with complaints about parking and about ALWAYS KEEP THE WALKWAY CLEAR and how smoking anywhere on the premises was in breach of the lease. Either this was Doug trying to make sure everyone knew how much of a pain in his ass they all were, or one of her neighbors was trying to point out that they all thought he was a pain in *their* asses.

She had been pretty alarmed when she'd first met Doug, but she didn't really have a choice at the time. Doug could throw up all the red flags he wanted; it didn't matter, because they needed an apartment that could salvage their move to Austin and they needed it fast, regardless of how tiny it was or how crazy the landlord, before Jack went completely over the edge and hitchhiked back to California by herself.

Ashley had received an email almost immediately after meeting Doug that proclaimed that he did NOT want to see their second car parked ANYWHERE on the property, or it would be TOWED and they would be

EVICTED. She'd had no idea what he was talking about—she and Jack had always shared a car, their shitty VW. But then she'd realized: Doug, this terrible man, could not imagine a world where two women—married to each other or not—shared anything together like a car or a last name or a bed.

Immediately after *that*, their next-door neighbor Mo had gone out of his way to warn them about Doug. "He's a bit of a loose cannon, that one," the older man had said with a wry smile. "Just keep your heads down and you should be fine."

Ash sighed. She'd keep her head down, no problem.

She stepped into the laundry room, and after she'd moved the damp pile of clothes out of the faulty dryer and back into a washer for a quick rinse, she paused at the doorway. Her eyes flitted to the left, down the walkway that led to the pool. Why was she hesitating? She couldn't actually believe Jack saw that same guy here, at their new apartment a good thirty-minute drive from that scene at the river, could she? It had been dark that night, and Jack was just hysterical.

But a part of Ash *wanted* to believe. A part of her would rather find the Cardigan Man here ready to jump out with a knife than find nobody and realize her wife could be losing it.

She's not "losing it." Trauma lives in the body, and this is Jack's trauma manifesting itself.

But still . . .

Just do it, Ash. Protect your wife like she protected you at the water.

It was that fact that pushed her to investigate: the fact of her shock when Jack pulled her away from the

Cardigan Man and took a fist to the boob. It had always been Ashley stepping forward in confrontations, Ashley shielding Jack from the real world then taking her home and having the hottest sex of their lives. But the force of the Cardigan Man's racism had rooted her in place, and Ashley had done nothing.

So do something now.

She walked out the other side of the breezeway, down the path that hugged the sloping hills of grass behind the apartment building. Past a fork that led to the pool's gate (where she'd recently deposited an inflatable wedding-ring float), the path continued its meandering way to the creek. On her right lay a row of canoes, kayaks, and other floating devices her neighbors took out on the water. Ashley had never been an outdoorsy type, but sometimes she wished she was. Part of her had thought their move to Austin could be the beginning of that, if it wasn't so hard to convince Jack to come along.

Today would be one of the last hot days of the year. She'd heard of the prodigious thunderstorms that rampaged through Texas all summer long, but had yet to witness one herself. Maybe one was coming on now. The change in the air gave her the impression of being inside instead of out, like she was in a vast cathedral; the canopy of trees soared above her like a vaulted ceiling. It filtered the light from the late-day sun. The effect somehow made her more aware of everything laid out before her, more appreciative of the sacred space. Usually she was so focused on the walkway ahead of her, lest she trip, that she barely saw everything else, but now . . . Ashley noticed branches in the walkway she'd never seen before, going down and around the far side of the pool and to little jetties at the edge of the water. She noticed strings of Christmas lights threaded from branch to branch, though she hadn't yet seen them lit. Clouds of midges danced (she'd hoped to see fireflies stitch seams in the air, though apparently this was the wrong time of year) and she felt the soft brush of shed caterpillar cocoons filtering down from the trees above and catching in her hair.

And here was the end of the walkway, sneaking upon you quick, after a few stretches where it was broken and uneven like clashing tectonic plates. Ashley stopped. The trees were too dense for her to clearly see the creek as it flowed past and grew into a broader expanse of water. But one thing was clear:

She could see no Cardigan Man.

She sighed, making her way back in the latening September air.

"Well, Ash," she muttered to herself. "Maybe your wife's just crazy."

3

JACQUELINE

"Hate crimes against Asian Americans increase 500% after President Trump calls COVID-19 'the Chinese disease.' "

—*The New York Times*
March 2020

"The question answered by this article's title is an age-old one that the advent of the internet has promulgated, most notably in all the crystal- and salt-littered corners of the 'woo-woo' world: 'Has anyone else been having weird dreams lately?' Metaphysical pseudoscience aside, in this new viral world the answer might finally be backed by experts. Alice Butler, a psychologist at Harvard Medical School who has spent the last four years studying dreams, explains that the mass anxiety and loss of circadian rhythm during America's COVID-19 crisis has given rise to what she calls 'REM density,' a kind of melting pot of the mind that is running in overdrive to work through its daily stresses. So, yes, you and the rest of the world are stuck in some kind of Freddy Krueger dreamscape. But also, no, quartz crystals and all the saging in the world will not help."

—"Yes, We're All Having Weird
Quarantine Dreams," Vox.com
March 2020

JACK DREAMT of the Cardigan Man.

She was in the front row of her BioChem class in high school. Which made no sense—she'd spent that entire semester in the back, not in the front like the teacher's apple-shining favorite. She'd hated that class, hated how Mr. Platt would stare so openly at her chest. He acted like she'd willed her body to mature faster than her peers' for his benefit alone, the way he smiled at her. To everyone else he was oh so charming, but to her he was an octopus waiting to *plop-plop-plop* his many-suckered tentacles around the curves of her hips and down to her ass.

But it wasn't Mr. Platt. It was the Cardigan Man.

There with the same smile as her old BioChem teacher was Good Ol' Mr. Cardigan Man Platt, popular with the kids, the *cool* teacher who was showing a movie during class. She focused on the image projected on the whiteboard, the Cardigan Man standing in the middle of the projection so that the image washed over him in confusing splotches. *Jaws*. The teacher was quizzing them on the themes of the blockbuster, on why it remained so relevant thirty-five years later, was quizzing Jacqueline specifically on what the final lines of the film were, but she didn't know and the class buzzed with whispers and giggles behind her.

The projection boiled away, disappearing in convalescing holes of flame, and now it was the Cardigan Man's face that was boiling, bulging out on one side. Jacqueline screamed. Mr. Cardigan Man laughed, smiling disarmingly at her, and said, "Relax, bitch, I'll cover it up. And then I'll cover you," and his arms *plop-plop-plopped* into elongated tentacles and split and replicated until they were everywhere.

He stepped closer, but Jacqueline couldn't move. She was older now, almost thirty, not a high schooler, but still she couldn't move, still she was stuck in the same spot after all these years, still under the control of Mr. Platt and the Cardigan Man and her parents and Ash and now she *was* Ash, frozen as the Cardigan Man lunged forward, but there was no Jacqueline behind her rushing to save her. He stepped closer and closer and one of his tentacles pulsed forward and dipped and slithered into the open maw of her backpack and came back out clutching something, an N95 respirator mask—*Hey, that's mine!*—but it flickered, changing its shape, switching from a nurse's mask to a gasmask to a hockey mask like the channels on a television. The tentacle placed the mask over the Cardigan Man's grotesque, boiling, undead face and he said:

"Do you know what day it is?"

"JACK!"

Heat spiked through her body. She jolted up, entangled in the sheets, panting.

"Hey, shhh, baby, shhh . . . just a dream . . . just a dumb dream . . ."

Ash sat on the edge of the bed and rubbed her back

in a soothing circle, but kept an arm's length away. She knew Jack needed physical space when she woke up like this—which was admittedly often—or else she'd feel claustrophobic.

"Shhh . . ." Ash didn't ask about the dream. She knew not to do that either. "Want me to close the blinds again?"

The blinds were still up from when Ash had come bounding in professing today as an early weekend, but the sun had climbed out of view, and it was a small window anyway, so it was relatively dark.

"No, I'm . . . what day is it?"

"I told you, silly, it's Friday! Friday the Thirteenth, actually, hardy har har. And it's already almost *three o'clock*."

"Shouldn't you be at work?"

Ash didn't reply, but there was something in her expression.

"What?"

Still she just sat there, frozen.

Jack's heart skipped a beat. A chill swept through her, and her sweat-coated skin was suddenly ice cold. "Did something happen?"

For another beat Ash's face was frozen, something unarticulated pushing heavily on her brow. And then she crumpled. Quivering lower lip, scrunched-up eyes, bursts of color in her cheeks. The tears flowed.

"Oh, Jack, I . . . I . . ."

Jacqueline scooched forward, sweeping Ash up in her arms. In this way they were polar opposites: Jack needed space, but when Ashley lost control of her emotions—which was rare—their dynamic completely switched. It was Jack's turn to soothe and calm and coddle.

Jack knew she could be a lot. She knew that at times she couldn't get out of her own way and needed someone's help. But she also knew Ash excelled at taking control. They were a great team in that way. They were also a great team in this way, because the few times this happened were special to Jack—almost sensual, in a way, because sometimes the hottest thing you could do was shut out the entire fucking world and say, *Hey, it's just us. It's just us.*

"It's just us, Ash, it's all right . . . just you and me."

Jack pressed Ash's sobbing face against her chest and held her close, rocking her back and forth, and hummed to her. Nothing came to mind at first and it was just tuneless *hmmms*, but then it took shape and she realized—

"Hmm-mmm . . . hmm-dnn . . . dun dun dun dun . . ."

—she'd somehow fallen into a weird, atonal version of the theme from *Jaws*, her brain and her vocal cords in a tug-of-war over whether it should be in a major or minor key. She forced herself to break the pattern and cut herself off, just shushing and holding and rocking and kissing the part in Ash's hair.

But now came the part she hated. Even though Ash usually, for Jack's sake, suppressed her need to constantly talk through things (or write them out in all those journals of hers), now was a time when she needed that most. Jack hated wading through the stagnant pools of cave water where things like relationship problems and suppressed traumatic memories and *icky feelings* dwelt.

But now she said, "Shhh . . . you can tell me, babe. Whatever it is. What happened? Did someone die?"

Ash laughed, snorting through the tears and snot. Death was the first thing that had flashed through Jack's mind, but she realized now how silly that was. Ash wouldn't have let Jack sleep through the day if someone had died—and she definitely wouldn't have pretended she was staying home from work for an early weekend of partying.

"Your job?"

Ash's laughter crumbled into another sob.

That was answer enough.

"I thought you said you just landed them their biggest client ever. Like, Exxon or someone. Why would they *fire* you?"

"They . . . they"—big, shuddering breaths—"they fired *everyone.*"

Ash sank deeper into Jack, but Jack just sat there, numb.

Everyone?

"That makes no sense. Exxon just—"

"Jack, forget it. Exxon's dead."

You said nobody died.

"Dead?"

Ash sat up, wiping her face on her tank top. "Exxon announced nationwide closures this morning. The same as, like, a dozen other giant corporations. The stock market's plummeted."

"You lost your job because of the stock market?"

"No, I—"

A flash of frustration, which only frustrated Jack. She was talking through this shit for *Ash's* benefit, not her own, so what gave Ash the right to be frustrated with *questions*? Although, this wasn't just for Ash now. Jack was confused. That heat from her nightmare was rising to the surface again.

"I think maybe you need to see the news, Jack."

She looked at Ash's red, cried-out face.

The news . . . ?

She followed her wife into the other room, to the TV.

And heard the President of the United States speak directly to her fear.

THE FEAR HAD FOLLOWED HER for years. Maybe her whole life.

Maybe when she first looked out across the playground at her friend Bethany and felt her face blush from a confusing rush of joy, wanting to run up and squeeze her friend until she squealed with delight. Maybe later that very night, as she lay in bed, wondering what Jesus was thinking as he read her thoughts about Bethany. Was he mad? Would he tell her parents?

Maybe when she first told her crush that she liked them. It was high school. Sarah Jenkins had looked at her like she was a cockroach climbing from a garbage heap and said, "You're not gay, so I know you're just making fun. Fuck you, Jack." The sting of those words was like a barb to the heart, and then was followed by years of confusion, of looking at herself in the mirror and being afraid that she didn't even know the person looking back.

Maybe when she tried to commit suicide. The fear then had been stalking her for years and was so close that it was breathing down her neck, a darkling demon, whispering to her that she was a liar and that everyone knew it. But in the end the fear of waking up in a lake of fire in the bowels of the earth was stronger than the other fears and the razor had slipped in her hand.

The fear had stalked Jack to the bar where she'd met Ash. It had stalked her all the way through their wedding, and then made the long trek from the west coast to the state of Texas, hot on her heels yet always just out of sight so that she'd question herself, question her own sanity, question what others told her, even Ash, or maybe especially Ash. Question her own fucking shadow.

And Jack couldn't stop it. She couldn't tamp down the fear.

The fear was back now. It had found her as she stood in front of the TV with Ash, her T-shirt still damp from her fevered nightmare and from Ash's snot and tears. The fear rose with every word and image and tickertape phrase that made her think of the Doomsday text of her mother's Bible.

A virus.

The virus.

"I told you this would happen."

Her breath was hot on her tongue. Barely a rasp.

She swallowed. Her throat just gave a dry *click*.

"I *told* you this would happen," Jack said louder.

They still stood side by side, staring at the TV, at the President, who for some reason was now going on about—what? It was hard to tell. Ratings? Responsibility? The last administration? It didn't matter. What was important was that Jacqueline had already predicted this would happen and had told Ashley *months* ago.

"Baby, I didn't know," Ash said, her voice small. "How was I supposed—"

"You were supposed to believe your wife. But you never *believe* me! You never believed what I told you about this virus, you never believed me about the Cardigan

Man—"

"*Oh, stop it with the Cardigan Man. He's not here, he's not around every corner, he's not fucking Pennywise!*"

Though neither of them had turned to face the other, Ash's voice had climbed an octave. She only ever spoke that high in her baby voice that Jack thought was so cute. This wasn't cute. This was an accusation. This was confirmation of her fear.

Ash thought Jack was crazy.

But she had *proof* now that she wasn't. The news confirmed it!

"Ashley. I told you back in December that this was going to escalate. I told you all about how the novel coronavirus could mutate—"

"You're not a fucking biochemist!"

"—and I told you we needed to prepare for when it reached this country. I told you, I said we'd need power and dry food storage and—"

"Oh, like I was going to just become a hoarder or a fucking prepper because of your *paranoia*—"

Silence. That final word hit them both like a slap. Even Ash looked surprised at what she'd said. The television droned on, but they'd turned away from it to face each other in the heat of their argument and now it was nothing but an insect's buzz in Jack's ears.

Paranoia. A taboo word between them. A loaded gun they'd taken off the mantelpiece in unspoken agreement, never to be used and *especially* never to be used as ammunition in a fight.

Jack spoke calmly: "I'm not paranoid."

Ashley nodded, her face flush. "Yes—oh, Jack, I'm so sorry—"

"I'm not paranoid. I'm *right*."

"Baby . . ." Ash's eyes were pleading. "You're right—you're *right*. And I am so sorry I didn't listen to you. I didn't know how legit all this"—she gestured at the TV—"was—"

"I *told you* how legitimate it was."

"You did, you did, but I didn't know if you were just . . . worrying like you do—"

"That's a cop-out and you know it. You didn't *want* to believe me, you didn't want to believe anything like this could come out of where you came from."

Ash blinked, her eyes widening, her mouth a perfect *O*.

"Where I came from?"

"I . . ." Jack looked away. "Come on, I didn't mean it like that."

Ash stepped back, her foot brushing the pile of bills next to the couch.

"Where did I come from, Jack?"

When Jack didn't speak—*couldn't* speak—Ash grabbed the remote in a burst of pent-up energy and muted the TV, the images still miming disaster.

"Tell me where I came from, Jack."

"I . . ."

Ash stepped toward her, tossing the remote to the couch.

"Los Angeles. California."

Jack closed her mouth.

"But you're not saying this deadly virus came from LA, are you, Jack?" The venom in her tone was unmistakable. "You're saying it came from people who look like me. Because people who look like me are dirty and yellow and crawling with disease. People who look like me eat bats and shit, right?"

A silent tear fell down Jack's cheek. "I'm sorry. That's not what I meant."

Ash took a deep breath, then another. "I don't have time to unpack what you meant. You said you're sorry, I said I'm sorry, we both said shit we didn't mean, and we love each other."

Jack nodded emphatically, another tear falling, and gasped with relief.

"The point is, we're in real trouble, and I'm not just talking about what's happening out there." Ash pointed out the wide sliding-door window. "National shutdown means a lot of businesses are done, over, just like that. And the ones that aren't are the ones that can keep running remotely, with their employees in the relative safety of their own homes. Which is a real problem for *me*, since I'm a sales rep for a company that sells commuting services to corporations. Or *was*. The job's gone, babe."

A flash of guilt strobed Jack's vision: the stale art supplies dumped unceremoniously over the beat-up yoga mat in their bedroom, the months and months to set up her Etsy shop that still had no customers. She'd done nothing. Here she was yelling at Ash for not prepping their food supplies for the coming virus and she had not been prepared herself. She should have known paying jobs would be scattershot and unreliable when this hit. She should have actually done what she'd said she would do when they decided to move to Texas. She should have prepared.

Jack's dream rushed back to her: a teenager again, sitting in a classroom, unprepared for the pop quiz.

"But maybe that won't matter," Ash continued. "Maybe I can find a new job fast, get ahead of this, find a sales position that will still exist with all this craziness going on. But that might take time. So our first step is to make sure we have enough food for when public panic hits critical."

Hits critical? Jack thought. She said, "It probably already has."

Ash nodded. "Not as panicky as it *will* be. Not if I don't move fast. I should have done this hours ago."

Jack looked at Ash, surprised. "Done what?"

Ash blinked. "We need food, babe."

"You just got groceries, didn't you? Ash, you can't honestly be thinking about going out there. Not with—"

Not with death in the air, she didn't say.

Her dream rushed crystal-clear to the front of her mind, playing across her eyes like the *Jaws* projection across the Cardigan Man. She saw his face overboiling from behind his mask—except now it was a gasmask—his skin peeling away with disease and revealing the skull underneath. Its grinning, masked face asked, *Do you know what day it is?*

Jack thought: *It's the day my wife contracts a deadly virus and brings it home to me.*

But she couldn't say this. After their fight, after saying such awful things to each other, they existed in a marriage bubble. They both knew it would pop if they continued this fight, so they both handled their words with care.

Instead, Jack heard herself say, "Need me to come with?"

It was so absurd, the idea of Jack, *paranoid* Jack, stepping out into a pandemic. But Jack had said it nonetheless, because she felt sorry for the hurtful things she'd said.

Ash, who also felt sorry for the hurtful things *she'd* said, replied, "I can move quicker on my own, but thank you."

And Jack watched helplessly as her wife changed her shirt and washed the redness and tears from her face, as she slipped on shoes and grabbed the keys, as she stepped outside and closed the door, staying quiet the entire time, not wanting to burst the bubble of their marriage, but her mind screaming:

Don't go, Ash, don't leave me, don't go!

And, most terrifying of all:

You'll get sick! You'll get both of us sick!

4

ASHLEY &
JACQUELINE

Legit saw 2 adults fighting over the last TP today. & then theres that asshole who stockpiled
Purell so he could price gouge. We deserve
whats coming. We are the virus. #coronavirus
#fuck2020 #stayinside

@AreYouFuckingKiddingMe

4:20 PM · March 13, 2020

7.7K RTs 39.5K likes

WITH ONE LAST, long blat of her horn, Ash screeched
into the parking spot.

"Fucking *finally*!"

HONK!

She displayed her middle finger to the car in her rearview mirror. "Fuck off, asshole!"

But he didn't, not right away, and just when she was
starting to worry that the big-ass Ford F-150 behind her
wasn't going to leave—that maybe she shouldn't have
been so quick to give in to road rage in a state with open
carry—it drove off. The big bearded guy leaned out his

window and shouted "Fuck off my land!" at her.

Ashley's heart pounded. She calmed herself with some deep breaths and checked the time.

4:20 p.m.

Which meant it had taken her a full hour to drive maybe three miles and navigate this crowded parking lot.

Her mind flashed at the time again. *Four twenty—damn, I miss California right now.* A little THC oil to calm the nerves would be perfect, with all the chaos she was about to walk into. But then again, maybe it was a good thing she'd left all that behind—getting high right now would just slow her down.

Her mom had called her five times today already, and ignoring every call was starting to give her anxiety. Ash would just keep her phone stuffed in her pocket, on silent. And then there was Jack, who would also be blowing up her phone every five minutes asking if she was still alive.

Jack . . .

Ash would pay for that "paranoid" comment back at the apartment, she knew it. Part of Jack's paranoia was thinking everyone in her life *knew* she was paranoid, which meant even mentioning it sent her into hysterics. And somehow Ashley had managed to let it slip on the first day of the apocalypse.

"Way to go, Ash."

She checked herself in the rearview—the tears and snot were all gone, but her eyes were still pretty puffy and she didn't have any eyedrops in the car, but fuck it, nobody was going to be looking at her anyway.

* * *

JACK WAITED.

She sat with her back to the sliding-door window, her knees pulled up tight, her phone sitting on the floor, face up, ready to light up with a text or call from Ash if something went wrong. Still, every few minutes she couldn't help but stab her finger at the phone to wake it up and see what time it was. As she did now for the hundredth time.

The screen read 4:20. An hour.

"Where are you, Ash?"

She said this aloud and then cringed at her own voice. *Talking when you're alone . . . that's what crazy people do.*

Maybe she was crazy. But she'd just had a fight with Ash in which she's said something *racist*—something Ash was supposed to trust she'd at least never have to face with Jack. Her wife's expression when the words flew from Jack's mouth, that slapped surprise in the eyes, how her little mouth had stretched into a perfect *O* . . .

And now she was out there, outside during a goddamn pandemic.

What if something happened and she didn't come back?

What if that fight was their last conversation?

Maybe Jack should go after her. Show her she cares, help her get through the craziness that was surely waiting for her at the H-E-B. She could get an Uber—

She almost choked on her laughter when she realized what she was considering.

"Go out there, Jack?" she said aloud again. "You? You *are* crazy."

* * *

BUT ONCE ASH got into the H-E-B, things were weirdly . . . okay.

The parking lot had been like a surreal game of Frogger, speedwalking across it in fits and bursts so the constant stream of cars didn't hit her or honk at her or rush by before she could start to cross. It had been hopeless trying to get one of the carts people had ditched before someone else snatched it up—but then, Ashley wasn't sure she wanted to put her hands on a surface possibly hundreds of people had imprinted with their germs. That was the still, small voice of her paranoid wife speaking to her, telling her she'd catch the virus and bring it home and their deaths would be on her germ-crawling hands. Thus, even when she managed to find a discarded grocery basket just inside, by the claw machine full of stuffed animals, she didn't pick it up until she'd rescued a tissue from the emergency Kleenex in her purse (more like the "in case of the emergency of a publicly screaming, germaphobe wife" Kleenex) and used it as a buffer between her hand and the basket's handles.

But then, once she'd recovered from the hectic rush of getting inside, Ash paused, looking out over the store teeming with customers, surprised.

Ash was struck by how incongruously quiet it was. People moved in a thousand directions, yes, but the panic seemed to have been left at the door. It was surprisingly orderly, focused, as if the neighborhood had rehearsed for such a day, like a graceful fire drill. There was something else about the silence that she couldn't put her finger on. People seemed to be acting nice toward one another, actually *nice*. This was most incongruous of all, after her nearly violent battle for a parking spot just a hundred yards away.

She joined the calm flow of people and found herself neatly deposited in the bread aisle. Or, at least, she *thought* it was the bread aisle, though it was hard to tell. The shelves—nearly the entire store, it seemed—were practically bare. A spike of panic: Had she sat in raging traffic for an hour for nothing? But Ash pushed that thought down, looking around and reassuring herself that there would surely be enough for her to at least fill this basket. Jack had been right: they *had* just gotten groceries; this trip was just to top off the reserves so they could safely bunker down and wait out the first wave of the pandemic.

On closer inspection, it seemed that the H-E-B employees who were unfairly tasked with keeping these shelves stocked had made compromises. In the interest of time—or perhaps in the interest of not being trampled by panicked customers—any sense of organization had been forfeited. This may have been the bread aisle once upon a coronavirus-free world, but now it also held syrup, beef jerky, a few types of candy, and, on one shelf, absurdly, boxes of popsicles which were undoubtedly melted.

She plucked a few items here and there as she went, since the constant flow of consumers made it tricky to stop and consider what was on the shelves, but then she spied something up ahead that made her brain yell, *Get that! Get that, Ash!* At times like these her shortness made it difficult for her to navigate large crowds—Jacqueline's height of five-foot-nine was such a turn-on for her for that very reason—but in this moment it came in handy. Ahead, on the bottom shelf and tucked toward the back, was a big bag and a few cans hidden from view. When she got there and squatted down, she realized it was white rice and a few cans of beans. She quickly swiped the items into her basket before others spotted her treasure trove.

As she joined the rest of the shoppers once again, she heard an old man behind her humming a song under his breath. It tickled something in her brain. What was it? Of course: Toto's "Africa." The earworm to rule them all. It reminded her absurdly of a comedy routine about killing yourself in a grocery store (who was the comic? Patton Oswalt?) . . . but no, that wasn't the cause of the brain-tickle.

The silence.

She stopped in her tracks. That was it. It wasn't just customers who were oddly quiet. The store itself wasn't talking. No crackle of the intercom, but also, and for some reason far more indicative of *times, they are a-changin'*, no canned Muzak or '80s earworms like "Africa" or "Sweet Dreams (Are Made of This)" or "Everybody Wants to Rule the World."

The humming old man stopped behind her.

"Excuse me, young lady."

She kept walking. "Yes, sorry."

"No need to apologize. Strange times, huh?"

And then he resumed humming the music of an old world.

4:45 P.M. AND NO CALL or text or sign of life from her wife.

"Bitch is probably dead," the Cardigan Man said.

"Shut up," Jack said back.

"Why else hasn't she called? Or even texted?"

"Shut up, shut up, shut *up*—"

"I guess it could be she's still mad about what you said . . ."

"You're not real, you're not real, you're not real—"

"I mean, 'where you came from'? I guess you secretly agreed with me when I said she should go back to her country."

Jack clamped her hands over her ears, violently shaking her head.

The Cardigan Man knelt down, peering at her from the walk-in closet's doorway with his watchful demon eyes. She'd finally gotten up from the living room floor, unable to stay with her back against the sliding-door window's glass. She knew it was teeming with all kinds of creepies and crawlies just on the other side of the pane, trying to find their way in so they could squirm up her nasal cavity and lay their eggs just behind her eyeballs and their babies would pull apart the spools of her brain and reanimate her corpse in an insectile dance—

4:46. Still no call. Not even a text.

So she'd climbed into the walk-in closet of their bedroom and found safety in the heavy fabrics of the clothes hanging from the racks. She'd slid behind them and rested her back against the wall. It was the one place she'd always been able to feel safe. Something about feeling closed-in . . . snug . . . like she was in a cocoon.

It didn't feel safe today. Today, the Cardigan Man had still somehow found her. He squatted at the entrance and she just knew he was grinning behind that gasmask.

He took his time undoing the clasp at his throat and temple, and then peeled the mask away so that it hung at an odd angle. Somehow his voice was still muffled.

"You were right to be afraid of her. This sickness came from China. Where do you think your wife came from?"

"My wife comes from *Los Angeles*," she hissed back.

He chuckled, and it turned into a guttural cough, and she wished he'd put the gasmask back on. "Disease doesn't care about being politically correct, Jackie boy. And neither will the panicking Texans at your local H-E-B when they see Ashley's puffy Chinese face."

Puffy? "Ash hasn't even *been* to China—"

"A face that *you* made red and puffy by saying such horrible things. To your own wife, Jackie boy? How could you?"

"I didn't—"

But she had. She sent Ash to a public place after making her cry, and now all people would see was a face they associated with this pandemic's Ground Zero. They would fear the red, swollen signs of a possible sickness on that face . . .

"They're gonna attack her, Jackie boy," the Cardigan Man breathed. "Believe me, I know mob psychology. She won't last five minutes. What time is it?"

She glanced at her phone. 4:47.

He laughed, his eyes dancing with the fire that boiled his face. "She's already dead."

Jack put her face in her hands, her mind screaming.

The Cardigan Man whispered, "And you did *nothing*."

SHOULD PROBABLY CHECK your phone, Ash.

Things were moving too quickly for her to keep checking the time, but she was sure Jack would be freaking out by now. She felt guilty at thinking how predictably boring her wife's mental health had become since moving here, but that was the truth. Tiresome, a constant tax on her own energy. Ash had always been the cheerleader of fun in every group she gravitated toward (which were many, as a social butterfly), and so at first that dynamic had really worked in their relationship. Their yin and yang were a nice balance. But then, as the years progressed, Ash began to see how so much of her cheerleading was really just her trying to distract Jack from herself and the issues she refused to deal with. If she *didn't* distract her, and Jack was allowed to wallow in her thoughts and insecurities and fears, Ash would find herself facing a façade of indifference Jack put up to hide what lay deeper: resentment. Resentment at Ash for not being a dancing monkey of distraction or for not constantly reassuring her that, yes, she was attractive to queer women, and, no, everyone around them wasn't giving her dirty looks.

Right now, Jack would be freaking out about Ash's long absence—probably in the safety of their walk-in closet—thinking her deepest fears were confirmed and her wife thought she was paranoid and probably hated her for it and was leaving her now and never coming back.

Or maybe she's just worried about your safety, asshole.

Ash sighed and pushed all that from her mind, instead humming another supermarket mainstay that could have been playing right now if the H-E-B weren't so eerily quiet: "Never Gonna Give You Up."

As she hummed, her eyes wandered higher. Taking food from the lower shelves because of her height had worked well. There was still plenty of food down there, but her basket was overflowing with as much food as she could carry, and it was time to hunt out the registers.

As she circled the aisles back toward the front, she spied a curious thing: a shopper standing still in the melee. It was an old man, the same old man who hummed Toto behind her in the bread aisle. He was at least in his eighties, though she would have put money on older than that. A hunched-over white elderly gentleman with no basket or cart, standing among the rushing shoppers and staring around in confusion.

Ash came closer on her way to the registers, telling herself to ignore him, to focus on her own groceries so she could get out of this mess and home. But he looked up as she passed and they made eye contact. The lost expression shining back at her just about broke her heart.

She stopped. "Can I help you with something, sir?"

"I . . ." He seemed startled she'd spoken to him, and his grip closed imperceptibly on the single can of broth clutched to his chest. "I don't seem to . . ." He cleared his throat, and this shook some of that confusion from his eyes. "My wife needs incontinence supplies, ma'am."

Ashley blushed. Diapers. This poor man was looking for adult diapers for his wife. Of all the things to wade into a pandemic for. She hadn't seen a single worker in the aisles the whole time inside, but she knew this man was on the wrong end of the store.

Here you go, Ash, helping people instead of yourself.

Maybe that was why she'd stayed with Jack. Because some part of her needed to be needed and Jack undoubtedly needed her.

Why I "stayed"? Jesus, Ash, how could you think—?

She shook those thoughts away and smiled kindly at the old man. "You've got yourself on the wrong end of the store, I'm afraid. Why don't you follow me?"

"I . . . yes, okay," he said, though he still looked lost. "Very kind of you . . ."

"Not at all. I was going that way anyway."

This was obviously a lie, as she led him in the exact opposite direction she'd been heading. She looped around the back of the store and to the other end, checking to make sure he was keeping up with her. She'd just deposit him in the right aisle and continue her loop until she hit the registers.

But when they got there, it was an utter wasteland. Ash had skipped this entire section of the store, just focusing on the food aisles, so she hadn't realized that many of the shoppers must have come here strictly for toilet paper and cases of water bottles.

"Okay, sir, what you're looking for should be somewhere . . ."

"Thank you, young lady," he said, shuffling up the aisle to catch up with her. "I'm sure I can find Doris's things from here."

She almost left him then, to go find the registers, but there was that voice:

Help him, Ash . . .

Followed by the still, small voice of her wife:

Is that how you look at me, too? Helpless? Incontinent?

She told that voice to shush, told herself that she wouldn't one day be this old man wandering through the supermarket looking for adult diapers for a bed-ridden Jack, and planted herself there. "I'm sure we can find something in all this mess." She gestured at the aisle, which looked as though a hurricane had torn through it, half-opened paper products strewn about the mostly empty shelves. "Here, come with me."

She stepped toward him and brought her hand to his arm, which was wrapped in a wool sweater despite the relatively warm weather. The moment he had something to cling to besides his broth, his free hand clutching at Ash's, his expression relaxed. He gave her his first genuine smile, free of that lost glaze.

"You get away from him!"

There at the end of the aisle stood a middle-aged white lady with a finger pointing directly at Ash, as though she were warding against the Evil Eye.

Ash stopped, still half an aisle from the pointing lady. "Excuse me?"

But the lady didn't answer her. She turned to look past the aisles, toward the registers, and cupped her hands to shriek to the entire store:

"We've got an infected on aisle seven!"

Ash just gaped at her. *Infected?*

"I demand to speak to your manager!" the lady was still screaming. Except now one hand had left her mouth and fished a cell phone out of her voluminous purse. She turned her accusing eyes back on Ash. "I'm calling the police. You're not coming into my town and spreading your terrorist disease, you little bitch."

"Miss," the old man spoke up in his querulous voice. "She was just helping me. There's been a misunderstanding, and I'm sure—"

The woman had taken a few steps closer to them, and was now just a few feet away, brandishing her big-ass purse like a weapon and holding the phone to her ear.

"Yes," she said into the phone, ignoring the man. "I'd like to report a COVID-19 in progress."

" 'Report a COVID-19'?" The words were startled out of Ashley. She felt heat rise in her face. "Fuck you, I'm not sick just because I'm Asian, you racist bitch."

The old man's hand disappeared from her own and he pulled away. She turned away from the woman and saw horrified surprise in the old man's face. He was looking at Ash like he was seeing her for the first time, seeing the puffy red eyes from her cry session with Jack.

"No," she said. "I was just crying, I—"

Ash choked on the supreme ridiculousness of it all, of her trying to defend herself to strangers by explaining that she'd lost her job and she lived with a wife who was on the verge of agoraphobia, so breaking the news of the virus to her had taken a lot out of Ash. She shouldn't have to explain to these people that she'd cried because Jack wasn't the only one who was afraid, *she* was afraid, too, and—and—

She clamped her mouth shut. She watched as the old man backed away, frightened of her—of *Ash*, who was just trying to help him help his wife. She watched as he stumbled on a ripped-apart case of paper towels and gave a dramatic howl of alarm as he fell almost as if in slow motion and came to rest on his rump in the middle of the aisle.

"She just pushed down an elderly man!"

Ash whipped around. The woman was screeching into the phone about the bioterrorist who had struck her local H-E-B and who she claimed had just lashed out violently at an old man and would probably hold her down next and cough her "Chinese virus" into her face.

"No—I—I—"

"Yes, officer, I'll personally make sure she doesn't

leave my sight."

There was no talking herself out of this. If the cops were coming, who knew what *they'd* do? Not a single employee in sight to back her up, just this frightened old man and this fucking Karen claiming Ash was spreading an infectious disease. She had no delusions about what country she lived in. She didn't think the Texas ID in her wallet would prove shit in the eyes of the local trigger-happy cops.

"Move," Ash said coldly.

"Oh, no, you don't, this is a citizen's arrest—"

God, shut the fuck up.

Ash tried a different tact: "Move or I'll cough on you."

The look of abject horror that crossed the woman's face gave Ash a thrill of satisfaction. But, to the woman's credit, she held her ground, brandishing her huge purse like Captain America's shield.

Ashley didn't actually intend on coughing—all of this racist "the Asian girl must have it" nonsense needed to stop—but she did charge forward, hoping to at least scare the woman off. The lady had a solid fifty pounds on her, but Ash could scrap when she needed to. And just as she'd hoped, the lady jumped back with a little squeak of surprise, like leaping on a chair to avoid a little mouse. But before she was free of the aisle, Ash felt a tug and looked back. The fucking Karen had regained enough indignation to grab out and successfully catch her grocery basket, and now she and Ash were playing tug-of-war with it, the Kleenex in Ash's hand now shredded and useless.

"I'M BEING ATTACKED!" the woman screamed. *"HELP ME, HELP ME, THIS CRAZED FOREIGNER*

IS STEALING MY FOOD!"

"Jesus, lady, this is *my* basket and you know it."

"Don't you put the Lord's name in your dirty mouth."

Ash looked around, still holding on to the basket. This part of the store had remained surprisingly empty this whole time, but now she could hear others coming. She wasn't willing to wait and see if they'd be helpful or just make a shitty situation worse.

"Fine," she said, smiling at the woman. "Steal from a stranger, that's the Christian way for sure, lady." She let go of the basket, not waiting to watch the woman over-balance and fall on her ass as Ash charged out of the aisle to the nearest exit.

That's what you get, Ash, always trying to help someone else.

5

JACQUELINE

So Mitt Romney is a socialist now. If that's not
proof of the apocalypse, I don't know what is.
#coronavirus #fuck2020 #apocalypsenow
@DevinCow
5:46 PM · March 13, 2020
3K RTs 12.3K likes

JACK HAD TO DO SOMETHING.

The fear had always stalked her, yes, but her wife had
kept it at bay. Now Ash was gone and maybe wasn't coming back unless she, unless *Jack*, did something about it.
This was the new world, not the old one where she could
sit and wait for her wife to come and pick her up off the
floor and dust her off and wipe her tears and kiss her
booboos. This was a national crisis—a *worldwide* crisis—
and they'd never lived through something like this. Had
their parents or even their grandparents lived through
something like this? Maybe Ash's, but Jack's? Maybe.
Maybe not. The death toll in the United States that would
come from this virus would climb and climb until it was
like a death knell from the Liberty Bell itself. And then a

recession like this country had never seen. And then fear-mongering and dick-measuring from the lunatics in the White House who just so happened to have access to the nuclear codes. And it would be left to people like Jack and Ash to be the *new* Greatest Generation and fight back.

Which meant getting out of this goddamn closet.

"You're not here," she said aloud to the Cardigan Man.

He laughed. "Whatever you say, Jackie boy."

But when she finally took her face out of her hands, she found that it *was* whatever she said. She'd said he wasn't here and sure enough it was just her, just Jacqueline, alone in the walk-in closet on a Friday afternoon.

Or evening. How late was it? How long had Ash been gone?

"And you did *nothing*," the Cardigan Man had said. Or no—her *imagination* had said. *You did nothing.*

But that didn't have to be true.

She clawed her way out of the curtain of hanging clothes and crawled out of the closet, using the mattress to pull herself up, and why did she feel so weak all of a sudden? It was her body shutting itself down because it knew what was coming, knew what she planned to do, and it refused. Her body was in survival mode.

"I'm coming, Ash," she said aloud, said more to her own body than to her absent wife, and left the bedroom to find her phone. She'd left it by the sliding-door window. As she scooped it up from the carpet, Jack averted her gaze from that window, lest she see what she knew was there: bugs, trying to get inside. Get inside her home and then inside her skull.

And now she was going outside?

"Yes," she insisted.

Before she could think further about it, she opened the Uber app and requested a ride. A driver accepted immediately, and she almost threw the phone, but then the driver canceled and she was shamefully relieved. Why had they canceled? The car on the app's little GPS map was near the H-E-B she knew Ash had gone to—maybe traffic there was backed up? Maybe that was why it was taking Ash so long in the first place. Maybe she was actually completely fine and would burst through that front door with arms full of groceries, exclaiming about the insane traffic.

No. It was Day One of a pandemic. The Uber driver had canceled because they didn't want to get sick and die. *Duh, Jack,* she told herself, again feeling ashamed of her relief at not having to go outside.

But then another driver, this one closer and coming from the opposite direction, accepted, and she had to suppress a scream.

You can do this, you can do this, you can do this.

"You can do this, Jack."

"You sure about that, Jackie boy?"

She looked up from her phone, dreading what she would see, but she saw it nonetheless, like a car crash you can't look away from: between Jack and outside, the monster in her head, in a cardigan that was now burnt to rags and crusted with dry blood; his beard was just as burnt and bloody, barely hanging on with the strips of skin still clinging to his skull. The gasmask swung rakishly from one hand—his tentacles were gone, thank Jesus, those had only been in the dream—and he leaned casually against the inside of the front door.

"Seems to me that if you go out this door looking for Ash, you might as well bring a body bag in case you find her. Nah, make that two body bags, so that whoever finds *you* after that can slide you inside and drop you off at the morgue."

She wanted to turn away. Wanted to look anywhere but at this rotting, laughing corpse. Even the bug-infested window would have been a relief after this. But she didn't. Couldn't.

Stop being paranoid, Jack. For Ash.

"You're not here," she told him. "Fuck off to Neverland."

He just laughed louder; the sound of it shook from his chest like glass in a meat grinder. "Oh, you're finally doubting yourself now, huh? Finally thinking maybe your little chink wifey was right?"

Jack winced. A flood of memories hit her like a physical force: the day she'd let herself be talked into changing the laundry. That had been last September, almost six months ago, and she hadn't stepped outside since. Going down the rusted metal staircase, through the potted plant cover, around the corner to the laundry room—and halting as if at a brick wall, ice freezing the blood in her veins to a complete stop.

Someone stood on the other side of the apartment breezeway. Someone grinning and laughing amiably as he came back from the dock down by the water. Her vision tunneled, stripping away the community bulletin board to her right and the laundry room to her left, and homing in on the man coming closer.

The Cardigan Man.

She jolted back with a colossal effort, tripping

backward and around the corner. She was never sure if he had seen her before she slipped away. The tunnel vision broadened in a *whump-whump* of her thudding heart. The world around her shook with her heart's beating against her ribcage as it worked to shake the ice from her bloodstream. Jack thought maybe he'd made eye contact with her in that frozen second before she stumbled away, maybe there had been a twinkle of recognition in his eye . . . or maybe she had imagined that.

Maybe she'd imagined the whole thing. That was what Ash said.

"There was nobody out there, baby," Ash had said when she finally returned from switching the laundry—a simple task Jack had utterly failed. And Jack had been so relieved to see her safely return that she'd just nodded dumbly.

But when Jack had regained her composure, when they sat in the still barely furnished apartment eating take-out, she'd gained the confidence to say: "He was out there. I saw him."

Ash hadn't responded for a while, taking forever to chew her food as she considered what to say. Considered how to say, Jack was sure, *You're just being paranoid.*

But what she said wasn't that at all.

"I've been reading on trauma."

Jack stared down at her food. It was Chinese takeout, which always made her feel sick afterward. It was the grease. Too greasy. More greasy than her favorite meal, pan-fried chicken thighs. Favorite because it was easy to make with very little seasoning but still just so *tasty*. They hadn't had her favorite in a while.

"Trauma lives in the body," Ash went on. "Your

mind sees something and its traumatized sensors shoot your fight-or-flight response into overdrive. It can be a rush of heat through the body, or tunnel vision, or dizziness, or a panic attack, or any number of things."

Jack muttered down at her food, "You don't believe me."

"I do believe you, baby. I believe that your body saw exactly what you say you saw."

"You don't believe me."

"I *do*, Jack. But can you take a moment and believe *me*? Believe in the possibility that memory is fallible and unreliable and that our minds are constantly playing tricks on us and massaging our confirmation bias?"

Jack thought about this and said, "You think I wanted to see him."

"It doesn't matter what I think." Ash's voice sounded calm and compassionate. It sounded like it did when she read her wedding vows. "But that's my point. It doesn't matter what either of us think. What matters is that we take a second and consider other, more objective possibilities."

Still Jack didn't look up. "Like that I'm crazy."

"Like that there are a million people in this city and only a couple dozen apartments in this complex. Like that it was dark when that man assaulted you. Is it more likely that you ran into the same single person after only spending a few weeks in Texas . . . or that your body needs time to heal and so it sees your trauma in every jumping shadow?"

Every jumping shadow. That was a new one. It never ceased to amaze her all the ways the people in her life found to say "paranoid."

She felt her anger rise but knew it would only make her look ridiculous next to calm, compassionate Ash. So she just kept her eyes down and she ate, the chow mein tasting like it looked: intestines and living, squirming worms.

As the days went by, she'd felt silly. Ash had looked into the science behind this—how could her own, anecdotal certainty compete? (Ash loved that word, *anecdotal*. It never failed to make Jack feel insignificant, as though she couldn't even trust her own eyes. How was *that* for paranoid?) In the end, she slowly came around to Ash's way of thinking and berated herself: there was no "Cardigan Man" outside, she was just *jumping at shadows*, she was being a silly little girl ducking under the covers because the monster in the closet can't see you if you're under the covers.

Stupid, paranoid Jack.

But a little part of her—perhaps the stupid, paranoid part—couldn't let the possibility go. Even now, almost six months later, she couldn't ignore the possibility that after that late-summer screening of *Jaws*, after punching her and running off into the dark, that racist hipster with his beard and cardigan returned to his own apartment right here, where she and Ash had moved a week later.

"No," she said. "My wife *was* right. You're not here."

The Cardigan Man, still leaning against the front door, blocking her path to rescue Ash from the grocery store, chuckled deep in his glass-grinding chest. "Whatever helps you sleep at night."

"Fuck off," she said again. "You can't stop me."

He just grinned back.

She stepped forward. "It was August in Texas,

summer at the water. Who the fuck wears a cardigan?"

And she stepped forward again and again, until she thrust her hand through the dispersing mirage of her tormentor, and flung the front door open.

That done, she slipped on shoes, grabbed the spare key and her wallet, and rushed outside, glancing at her phone. The Uber driver was just two minutes away.

She passed a fire extinguisher clipped to the wall—this complex put all their fire extinguishers *outside* the apartments, which seemed pretty fucking stupid to Jack, and she'd begged Ash to bring it up with their landlord—and felt the urge to snatch it away and cling to its cold metal surface like a security blanket.

Don't be ridiculous, Jack, that's what crazy people do.

She charged onward, but then stopped at the top of the stairs. The air hit her like a fist of compressed air, a *whomp* that made her stop and look up. Something about the heavy gunmetal sky and the whipping winds spoke of the first ten minutes of every apocalyptic movie she'd ever seen.

You can do this. Go get Ash.

She pushed through the palpable doom in the air, her hair whipping into her face as she descended the stairs. The metal echoed under her feet.

The stairs formed a tight loop, climbing in ninety-degree turns, and though the corrugated metal frame left the surrounding area perfectly visible as you descended, some eccentric resident had taken it upon themself to dress the railings with potted plants and hanging vines. So, Jack could never see the ground level in that final turn and was always certain she'd run head-on into someone on their way up. Today was no different, though the added effect of dancing winds and today being the first day of a national emergency gave Jack a sense of . . . prescience. Certainty that she wouldn't like whatever waited for her at the bottom of the steps.

In that last moment before she turned to take the final echoing steps down, she was hit by a memory she'd nearly forgotten from grade school—kindergarten. One of five-year-old Jacqueline's classmates, Timmy, the biggest of the class, had decided that he was the Hug Monster, and had decided to give every other kindergartener on the playground a big bear hug. This terrified little Jacqueline. She fled in her terror, vaguely certain that a hug from a boy would make her daddy angry. Her daddy, who, just a few days before, had with flushed cheeks looked at her very seriously and said, "Jackie, Jesus sends girls who give themselves to boys straight to Hell." She had been afraid to ask what it meant to give yourself to somebody. Then, running through the playground, she'd turned a corner thinking she'd hide in the girls' bathroom—and ran straight into the arms of the Hug Monster. She smelled sweaty boy smell, and then he let her go because she'd burst into tears. Into hysterics.

She was going to Hell. She just *knew*. What if Daddy found out?

Now, hustling down the metal stairs, Jack felt a tingle on her skin at the memory of that day. Then she stepped down—

Straight into someone's open arms.

No, not open arms. This person bumped into her, just as unaware as she'd been. A tall man stumbled back, then looked at her and laughed.

CNN anchor: *The President of the United States has just*

confirmed that a respiratory transmitted virus has reached Americans. Please, if you can, stay inside and avoid all contact.

And the Cardigan Man's laughter.

Jack stared, frozen, at him, at the man she'd bumped into.

He laughed at her, recovered from his stumble. He wore a *Helter Skelter* T-shirt, not a cardigan, but the beard was the same as it had been back in August. So was that smile. He saw her cringe away and laughed harder. He spoke.

"Hey, I've been looking for you, neighbor! Wanted to give you a proper welcome."

He grabbed her. Grabbed her in his arms like the Hug Monster and swung her around. Slammed her against the apartment wall. A potted green something tickled her neck.

The sound of tires crunching gravel. Her Uber driver?

I should scream for help.

But she couldn't move. Couldn't breathe.

No gasmask, no burnt skin or grinning skull. But he was real.

"Where's your little girlfriend?" he asked. "She die of this virus thing already?"

She whimpered.

"Just being near you, I can feel my throat tickle. You make me want to . . . I've gotta . . ."

He coughed, that same guttural glass-grinding sound.

He coughed straight into her face.

She finally screamed.

He let her push him away. Chuckling, ambled down the corridor to the breezeway.

Her legs were rubber. She leaned heavily against the

wall, her eyes rolling in their sockets. She could feel it, that cough, sliming her cheek and neck and brow and lips—

It got inside her *mouth*. It was *alive*, it was a swarm of insects burrowing into her respiratory system and breeding inside of her.

"Jack, oh my god—"

Ash.

Jack managed to push out of her swoon and stand. Her legs felt watery, loose.

Ash was standing there, at the front of the gravel parking lot. Somehow Jack's brain made the connection—it was not her Uber driver, but her wife, finally back from the grocery store. But there were no groceries in her hands.

"Jack, ohmygod, it was *him*—"

Her voice was lost inside a *BOOM!* of thunder that shook their world. Rain fell then, fast and hard, but Jack was barely aware of it as she scrambled back up the stairs and to their front door, fumbling with the spare key.

Inside, she slammed the bolt home and pressed her back to the door. She slid down to the carpet.

She wept.

BOOM! BOOM! BOOM!

Not thunder. Her cries were strangled in her throat. The door shook against her back.

He was trying to get in. The Cardigan Man.

He would kill her.

BOOM! BOOM! BOOM!

"Jack, open up, please, it's me, I'm getting *soaked!*"

Ash's voice.

But could she trust it?

Sobbing again, Jack somehow found the strength to climb to her feet.

Another apocalyptic *BOOM!* of thunder.

"Jack, please!"

Jack turned and opened the door to her wife.

II

RISES

6

JACQUELINE

I love hearing conservative Christians talk about how they aren't going to let something invisible control their lives. #IsntItIronic #CanYouSeeMeLaughing

@TheTweetOfGod
7:06 AM · April 9, 2020
60.9K RTs 1.2M likes

JACK DREAMT she had been buried alive.

The musty smell of dirt was cut by the biting gag of decay hugging her body like a shroud. A dark more complete than her blackest nightmares pressed into her. She couldn't claw it from her skin. She couldn't claw it from the coffin. Her nails ripped from their beds in jagged stabs of pain as she clawed the splintery wood just inches above her face. Screaming, screaming, screaming. The last stab of pain before her fingertips grew numb was that of needlelike splinters decorating her hands like a porcupine's pelt—and then a deafening *SCHKKKG SCHKKKG SCHKKKG* as her fingers whittled themselves down to the bone, still scratching and scratching and scratching.

A change in the air. A change in the smell, in the taste of corrosive battery acid seeping down her throat, and she knew, she *knew*, that she wasn't alone anymore. Pushing itself through cracks in the shoddy carpentry, oozing down the walls of her coffin, was an alien sludge, a viscous snot hellbent on clogging her throat until her screams were nothing more than a moan . . .

"JACK!"

She burst through the barrier of sleep and woke screaming.

Ash's silhouette in the doorway. "Just a nightmare, babe. I'll bring you some water." She left, leaving Jack to the fear and the dirt on her tongue, the sweat slicking the sheets.

It had been one month since she had been outside.

7

ASHLEY

Crazy times, man . . . The cure for a pandemic might literally come from Tom Hanks's blood, yet meanwhile Tom Cruise went to China to preach Dianetics and no one's heard from him in over a month.

@ThisIsNotASatireAccountISwear
3:28 PM · April 1, 2020
1.1K RTs 20.5K likes

ASH'S SKIN CRAWLED with drops of sweat. Her heart jack-hammered dubstep against the cage of her chest. Her breath, deafening in her ears, was the rumbling rasp of a horror movie zombie overlaid with the juddering gasp of the slasher's final girl. But she couldn't stop. Had to do . . . just . . . one . . . *more* . . .

"Ten!"

Ash collapsed on the yoga mat. The dappled sunlight fell through the sliding-door window onto her body. After a pause, she lifted her head to look at where the light danced on her heaving abdomen. Was it just her wishful imagination or was she more toned than yesterday?

She pushed herself onto her side to stare out into the trees.

No one. Not a single person outside. Not even on the water.

As she cooled down from her last set of crunchies, Ash contemplated how surreal the last month had been. Locked up inside her tiny apartment, completely alone— at least she *felt* completely alone, though technically she still lived with someone—with nothing to gauge the real world but the images and doomscrolling on her laptop screen and television screen and smartphone screen. All her screens showed her proof of a world in chaos . . . and yet, the biggest screen of them all was this sliding-door window, and what it showed was a peaceful naturescape. It just didn't jive with Ash; she didn't *like* having a gorgeous view of the wonders of Mother Nature if it felt like a lie, like a papier-mâché mask. It was pretty, sure, but somehow false, a thin veneer behind which lay screaming white supremacists and hospitals overridden with rasping zombies and corpulent rapists pouting over nuclear weapons where their dicks should be. It was all *vu* and no *déjà*.

She sighed. "That doesn't even make sense, Ash."

She took a calming breath, let it out in a slow count of five, shifted to her knees, and started rolling up the yoga mat. This was her world, out here in the living room, with the antique-chest-turned-coffee-table pushed closer to the couch to give her this makeshift gym. She kept it clean and organized—unlike Jack's world in the bedroom. It was from that dark, dirty, unwashed world she'd rescued this yoga mat. It had taken a while to scrub off all the stains from Jack's moldering art supplies. But scraping away each layer of filth felt therapeutic, like shucking off that thin veneer to show the reality beneath. She imagined this mat as the screen of her life: not Jack's mess on the surface, but a simple, inch-thick mat on which Ash could exercise out the bad energy and exorcise out the worst juju.

Ash needed order, but even more than that, she needed to be the one in *control* of that order. That was why she was hot with sweat; it was why she had cleaned the yoga mat and wasn't just leaving it rolled out on the carpet in between uses. This was the small part of the world that she could control. Not the one out there, where a slow-moving government had decimated the country and put its economy back a hundred years, where the signs of a collapsed democracy reared their Hydra heads and spewed out a death count rivaling anything Ash's grandparents in Nationalist China had ever seen . . .

No, it was this living room that Ash controlled. It was this heaving body, sweat itching behind her shoulder blades and drenching her tank top, that obeyed her wishes. She could keep this room spotless and organized and designed in a way that created the greatest conduit for inner peace as she sat still and calmed her breathing. She could organize and catalog every item in the kitchen so that she had control over what she put in her body not just now, but for however long this self-quarantine may last. She could use the internet not to browse the horrifying news but to apply for job openings in tech sales. To update her résumé and to respond to potential interviews and to look up recipes.

Ash was in control of Ash.

But there was another part of the world where she

felt increasing lack of control.

Just down the hall and past the bedroom door.

Jack had always been a bit unstable, a little unpredictable—that was part of what drew Ash to her in the first place. It was exciting, like playing with an undiscovered isotope. But now all that had dialed up to eleven. Jacqueline hadn't left the dark sanctuary of the bedroom in a month. If their bathroom weren't connected to the walk-in closet in a weird open circle of hallway to bedroom to closet to bathroom to hallway again (another architectural anomaly courtesy of the '60s), Ash wouldn't have put it past her wife to go full animal and shit in the corner.

In a month, she hadn't spoken a single word. Hadn't even made eye contact.

THE LAST SHE'D DONE either of those things was in those terrifying moments of the first day of this nightmare, March 13—Friday the 13th, ha-ha oh so funny—when she'd finally let Ashley back inside the apartment. Thunder booming, lightning strobing down from barrel-chested clouds, hot rain pelting her back, Ash had stood frozen on their welcome mat as the door swung open for her. What would she see? Jack had just been assaulted in front of her eyes—assaulted by the very man whom Ash had sworn was just a figment of her overly paranoid imagination. Would she be angry? Sobbing?

She was much, much worse.

Jack's eyes blazed from her pale face, the whites showing more than her dilated pupils. Her hair was plastered down her forehead and over those eyes and yet they shone through, like searchlights pinning an escaped prisoner down on a moonlit prison yard. Her mouth hung open, spittle frothing from its corners, and her chest was unnaturally still, as though she weren't breathing.

And then her voice, the last two words she'd spoken aloud to her wife, a voice Ashley did not recognize. It was like a dream, like a dream strung together by seemingly unconnected bits of her waking reality, where you saw a friend but they talked with the voice of a stranger, or you came home only to find yourself somewhere you've never seen.

"Inside, quick."

Ash stepped over the threshold, out of the storm, and Jack was moving, slamming shut the door and throwing the bolt and locking the doorknob and pulling—no, *throwing*—the entryway table against the door.

And Ash heard herself speaking, though it was like talking to a stranger.

"Oh, Jack, baby, oh, fuck, I am so fucking sorry, did he—what did he—"

And Jack was gone, pushed past Ash and down the hall. But Ash would never forget that brief moment that stretched like taffy as Jack stepped past her: her wife, with those shining eyes swiveling lost in their sockets and that hanging, unbreathing mouth, shying her body away from Ash as she moved in the cramped space, as though this were a dream for her, too, as though she also didn't recognize this person the logic of the dream had insisted she let inside her home; as though she thought Ash had only gone to H-E-B to roll bodily in a vat of coronavirus agent and come back here to force her to suck it down and lick it from her fingers.

The bedroom door clicked shut, lost in the white

noise of the storm raging outside.

Ash remained by the entry, alone, her heart thudding in her ears. Tears pricked at her eyes, and as she stood in the sudden darkness of the twilit storm pulsing through the sliding-door window across the apartment, they rolled down her cheeks.

She waded through the hall and paused at the closed bedroom door, holding her breath. What would she hear? Crying, shrieking, swearing, pacing, punching pillows, what?

When it came, the sound was behind her, on the other side of the hall. It was the bathroom faucet. Jack had climbed through the walk-in closet and was now in the bathroom, scrubbing and scraping her skin. Then came retching and hawked spit and choked gasps, and then the sound of the bathtub faucet drowned all of that out.

Ash stood and listened for she didn't know how long. The sounds of the storm dimmed from her awareness. All she knew was inside that bathroom.

Eventually, in the dripping silence, Ash was aware that Jack had moved back to the bedroom. What was left was the muffled sound of a woman gently sobbing herself to sleep.

THE QUARANTINE HAD NOW lasted one month, and Jack had yet to step back out and into Ash's world. Just hours shut in the bathroom, the rest in the bedroom, melding into timeless catatonia.

Still, Ashley had tried to assert control over her marriage as well. In the weeks that followed that Friday, Ash had done her best to be a patient presence for Jack. She brought food to the bedroom—soups and oatmeal, mostly—though after having to throw out some of the spoiled meals she found on the bedroom floor, she only did so once a day. She'd failed to get groceries that first day, and didn't dare go out now, and anything she managed to order for delivery would either take weeks to arrive or not show up at all. They couldn't afford to waste food, and Jack wouldn't let her get close enough to spoon-feed her.

Ashley's phone pinged, bringing her back to the present. She grabbed the phone from the antique chest as she walked to the kitchen.

A series of texts from her mom.

Austin today. What if you need help and nobody comes?

This lovely sentiment along with a string of photos Ash's mom had found that showed downtown Austin. Sixth Street, deserted, entire buildings boarded up and tagged. Even the homeless population seemed to have dried up. Or gone elsewhere. To die, maybe?

She sighed. Placed the phone on the counter and filled the tea kettle with water to boil. Then texted back:

Our texts r still sending mom. i'll b fine. luv u

That was her mom's daily attempt, over and done with. Every day she'd gotten texts like this—sometimes phone calls, but Ash ignored those—trying to coerce her into coming home. Lists of airlines that were still flying out of Texas. Businesses that still delivered in her hometown. Entreaties from her father to come be with the family—though she suspected her mom made those up. Her father had been barely monosyllabic since the wedding.

As she waited for the water to boil, Ash jumped at her phone buzzing in her hand.

Now her mom was calling her. She ignored it, rolling her eyes.

As soon as the call went away, a text took its place:

My calls aren't getting through to you tho!

Ash sighed and quickly wrote back:

Yes they r, just shitty reception here, like i said a million times

The swear would hopefully do the trick and put her mom off her case at least until tomorrow. The "shitty reception" part was technically true. She could get texts, and calls would come through, but most of the time if she tried answering them it would just cut out after a few exchanged rounds of "What?" and "Can you hear me?" She'd meant to switch providers, but now . . .

Her phone buzzed again.

Mom, it said. Swearing hadn't scared her off after all. Well, she supposed she could answer and let the call drop. *That* would put an end to her mom's attempt to reach her today for sure, might even discourage her from calling more often.

She answered. "Hey, Mom. Can you hear me?"

"Perfectly, dear. I don't know *what* you mean about the reception."

Dammit. Her mom was right. Today of all days . . .

"Ashley, your father and I are worried about you."

"Mom, I'm *fine*. Jack and I are *fine*." Not technically true, but it always irked her how her mom managed to omit her daughter's wife from existence with just a few words. Ash was always inserting "Jack and I" into her sentences, and her mom was always studiously ignoring her.

Her mom said, "That city of yours isn't cheap, you know, and unemployed young people with no 401Ks shouldn't be expected to live through the upcoming recession by themselves. Your father says this one will be worse than the Great Depression."

That's what this was about. She should have known. Her mom had never liked her decision to move to a different state, but she'd be using this national crisis to her full advantage now to say, *I was right and you were wrong and now you can come crawling back home.*

The whistling kettle broke into her thoughts, and she didn't get in a response before her mother charged on. She turned off the gas stove as she listened and poured most of the kettle's contents into the filter and then into the glass carafe she kept chilled in the fridge. They were boiling all their drinking water now—or rather, *Ash* was boiling all their water now, though Jack would probably die of dehydration if she didn't. It was something to get used to when they first moved here: a massive late-summer rainstorm had flooded the water-treatment plant and the county issued a boil notice to its residence; months later, construction on the main line went wrong and in came another boil notice. Now, with everything as confusing and hectic as it was, Ash just knew Jack would expect the sickness to come in from the water pipes. So she had issued her own boil notice.

"I've prepared your old room," her mom was saying. "We can fly you home before they ground *all* the airlines, but we need to hurry." No crying, just her mother's own brand of fretting, somehow no-nonsense but still managing to fuss. Her mother had perfected this tone as she lorded over a young Ash yet still existed under her husband's thumb.

"Mom, Jack and I aren't leaving Austin, we *just* moved here! Besides," she said, racking her brains for ways to derail her mom's persistence, "no way would Jack and I fit together on that tiny twin bed in my room."

"Yes, well"—*yes, well,* her mother's go-to response to side-step having to actually acknowledge her own *Jack and I*—"your father and I can manage a single one-way ticket home, Ashley, so your bed would be just as sufficient as it was in high school."

"Mom, I . . ." She closed her mouth. Her mother had done it, had actually managed to shock her speechless. She hadn't expected *this*, such a brash conditional invitation. "Mom . . . are you seriously trying to tell me that *I'm* invited back home, but *my wife* isn't?"

"Your father, Ashley, he has rules. You know this." No hesitation whatsoever. "He has been gracious enough to allow that you can come home—"

"Oh, well, excuse me if I'm not properly *grateful* for Dad's kind-hearted slap in the face to his own daughter—"

"You never used to be like this, Ashley," her mom said suddenly, shutting her up. "What has she done to you."

Again, Ash was speechless.

"Your father and I want you home, dear," her mom said, charging ahead.

Finally, Ash managed, "Well, I'm sorry to disappoint, but you don't make the decisions for me. I'm sorry Dad has sent you to do his dirty work—"

"Oh, don't be so dramatic, I speak for myself."

Ash swallowed. "Keep telling yourself that. But you're done telling *me*."

"Ashley, dear—"

"Don't bother calling this number again, Mom."

And she hung up.

Hands shaking, she calmed herself by emptying the kettle into a mug and steeped a tea bag. Cradling the steaming tea, she stepped down the hall to the bedroom door.

She listened. Behind the closed door it was usually silent, but there would come the occasional coughing fit or indecipherable muttering. Ash spent almost no time in there herself—just enough to keep Jack fed and occasionally tell her things would be okay and that she loved her. She slept on the couch now, after several failed attempts at joining Jack. She didn't mind. Honestly it came as a relief when she finally decided she'd stop trying for something Jack so clearly didn't want.

Jack dreamed almost constantly now. The nightmares came every night, usually during the day, too, and it seemed they were getting more violent and caustic with time. Half the time Ash came into the bedroom not to collect dirty dishes but to wake and calm a screaming Jack.

No sound now.

She knocked. "Babe?"

Still no sound.

"I have tea."

She opened the door. A wave of fug hit her, and she wrinkled her nose involuntarily. A noxious Molotov cocktail of sweat and unwashed clothes and . . . something else. Fear? No. It was the smell Ash had come to think of as paranoia. Squirming, writhing spider's egg sac of paranoia, a mind so laden with the stuff that it exuded some kind of pheromone.

She breathed through her mouth and stepped inside the darkness.

"I brought tea, baby."

No answer from Jack.

"Chamomile. Maybe it'll help you rest."

Still no answer. Not even a restless ruffle of the blankets.

"Babe . . . ?"

She reached toward the shadowy bed, afraid of what she might find. She suddenly found herself wondering if there were any sharp objects in the bedroom—scissors, razor blades? Maybe she'd better hide them. Unless it was too late. Would there be blood under the blanket, so much of it that it refused to coagulate, seeping into the mattress and mixing with the yellow stain—

She flung the blanket to the side.

The bed was empty.

She stared around the dusky bedroom, her eyes bugging in her head as she tried to see into the shadowy corners.

"Jack?"

As she swung her head around the room, the mug jostled in her grip; hot water spilled onto her hand. She stepped over shadowy mounds of things so that she could place the mug down on the bedside table.

"Jackie, baby, you okay?"

Still, nothing.

Ash looked around the room as her eyes adjusted to the dim lighting. The place no longer resembled *their* bedroom, hers and Jack's. You couldn't see the framed *Jaws* poster or any of the floating shelves spaced around the wall. Mounds of discarded clothes and towels and blankets littered the floor. They were running low on quarters for the coin-op machines in the laundry room, and Ash wasn't sure what to do about that. Online she'd read that the US Federal Reserve had stopped issuing coins to banks, so quarters were already becoming a rare currency, like two-dollar bills. Who would have thought that in the apocalypse it was questions like "How am I going to do my laundry?" that were most pressing?

But the maybe-forever-dirty laundry wasn't the worst of the bedroom's chaos. Ash knew that those shadowy mounds were hiding the more grotesque items—the moldering food Ash had missed somehow, or Jack's flaking pastels and paints and clays, or wads of snotty tissues, or bug carcasses . . . or perhaps the bugs thrived in here, and weren't dead at all. That thought heralded a new image: the dim room's mess now resembled to Ash shadowy swaths of spiderwebs, like Shelob's lair as she lay in wait for the doomed hobbits . . .

Ash shook her head, trying not to laugh at her own ridiculousness. What would Jack think if she heard her laughing? She'd think Ash were laughing at *her*, laughing at how stupid and paranoid she was being.

And why shouldn't she think that? Ash thought. *After what I put her through . . .*

Ash suppressed a sigh. She wasn't sure she'd ever forgive herself.

That Friday the 13th—no, she'd never forgive herself for that day.

For leaving Jack alone after such a terrifying revelation, sure.

For not thinking to text Jack updates while she was away, sure.

For not even managing to come home with a single bag of groceries, yes.

For all of this culminating in Jack going outside and running into that man, yes.

That . . . Cardigan Man.

He *did* live here.

Jack had been right. Not paranoid, not overreacting, but *right*. For months.

And Ash hadn't believed her.

Worse, she'd *gaslit* Jack. All that "trauma lives in the body" nonsense was just code for a patronizing pat on the back and an "Are you sure you saw what you think you saw, because I don't think you did."

Here they were, far away from home, supposedly starting a new life, and it turned out Ash was no better than Jack's parents.

But she'd keep trying to make up for that. She was at least in control of what she did moving forward.

"Tea, Jack?"

The closet. Its door stood open. Jack sometimes liked to spend time in there. Something about the hanging clothes pressing into her made her feel safe.

But before Ash could check, an inhuman gasp came from past the closet's doorway.

Farther, through the closet and into the bathroom—

A bloodcurdling scream.

8

JACQUELINE

If even ONE American dies from Ebola then President Obama should apologize to the American people and RESIGN!

> @realDonaldTrump
> after the 2014 Ebola outbreak
> killed two Americans

The Do Nothing Democrats are a bunch of totalitariotismsts who are spreading FAKE NEWS about this Kung Flu. America in GREAT SHAPE!

> @realDonaldTrump
> the morning of 150,000 confirmed
> American COVID-19 deaths

AWAKE AND ASLEEP were no longer separate states of being for Jack. Not after that moment outside, pressed up against the building, a well-groomed beard and dazzling smile all that she could see. The Cardigan Man's rough hands pinned her like a bug in a display case and his face filled her vision and then he was coughing on her.

Whenever the moment replayed in her mind—over and over and *over* it played—he was heaving a cascade of vomit onto her, like a shower of chemical waste burying her in an alien sludge she would never claw her way out of . . . and then, like a dream, she was out and up and inside and *BOOM! BOOM! BOOM!* was the thunder of the door and against all the screamings of her mind she let someone inside, said *"Inside, quick,"* and she didn't even recognize her own voice, as though the chemical waste had scalded her tongue and morphed it into an alien slug that spoke for her—

That one moment, over and over. When awake. When sleeping. It didn't matter. The Cardigan Man's grinning face splitting open like a snake unhinging its jaw. A torrent of luminescent bile burying her alive. Her skin, her tongue, her very thoughts, all transforming under the power of whatever cosmic toxins melded into her body with his guttural cough.

It was a time loop she couldn't escape. Sometimes the loop grew to include other moments. She'd relive the night at the river, the feel of the Cardigan Man's fist as it sank into the flesh of her breast; weeks later, seeing him at her new home, at the other end of the breezeway like a clown looming at the mouth of the sewer; then questioning if she'd seen him at all, her wife's words spinning around her, *you see your trauma in every jumping shadow in every jumping shadow you jump at trauma in your every shadows . . .* but it always returned to that infinite moment under the rough hands of the Cardigan Man, cowering under the viral mist of his cough.

For some time she was aware of nothing else. Eventually she felt moments of lucidity. She'd wake to find herself in the bathroom, holding her hands beneath a rush of scalding sink water. Bottles of soap and toothpaste and mouthwash would be littered before her, and she'd have the thought, *Maybe the bleach would do it . . .*

And then right back into the time loop.

Sometimes the time loop would boil and bubble into a nightmare tangent. She'd be running through a playground that sprouted overnight behind her apartment complex, on the stretch of hill between the sliding-door windows of the apartments and the water below. Running through a playground that towered over her like it had when she was five. Gasping with a thrill of fear because she knew the Hug Monster was coming for her, in his cardigan and gasmask.

Or she'd have a lucid moment and find herself in front of the bathroom mirror—but staring back at her would be the Jacqueline from middle school. A ponytail pulled over one shoulder, a training bra fit over her torso for the first time. She was holding scissors, had come in here to cut off that ponytail because her dad had smiled down at her and said, "Little girls shouldn't need training bras," and so she didn't want to be a little girl anymore. But then, just as she was ready to cut the ponytail in one *snip*, a torrent of thoughts—

Bethany, her smile of sunshine. Jesus, in her head at night, saying, *My Father doesn't like what you're thinking, Jackie, and He's going to tell your father.* That night in her bed when she'd finally told Jesus to shut up and she stuffed her pillow between her legs and felt all tingly down there and somehow it made her think of Bethany's smile. At church next to her dad, reading the story of Mary, and wondering if somehow Timmy, the Hug Monster, had made her "with child" too.

Middle-school Jacqueline stared at the blades of the scissors reflected in the mirror. She stared as she brought their open mouth not to her ponytail but to her bared wrist, where a blue vein gently pulsed . . .

She stopped. Just then, she felt someone's . . . *presence*. The scissors hung inches from that gentle blue vein.

"Daddy?" she called.

No answer from outside the bathroom door. And yet she still felt that sense of being watched. Of being lorded over. It wasn't Jesus—she'd stopped thinking he was there years ago, had assumed he saw her thoughts about Bethany in grade school and abandoned her to sin and Hell. But she felt it like a hand hovering over the nape of her neck. A crawling, hair-raising tingle. She was suddenly sure that what watched her was in the tiny bathroom with her . . . what watched her wasn't human, wasn't visible . . . wasn't friendly.

And it *wanted* her to do it. It wanted to grin over her shoulder at her reflection as she pressed the sharp edge of one of the scissor blades to the thin skin below her palm. It wanted to chuckle and cough in amusement as she sawed the scissor mouth open and shut, open and shut, across her wrist, gouging and cutting until, like leaning against an electric fence, the metal teeth of the scissors caressed the strands of nerves hiding behind the muscle and bone and blood, plucked them like harp strings to produce the music of pain.

When she blinked, she wasn't in middle-school Jacqueline's bathroom anymore. She was back in Texas, back in the pandemic, in adult Jack's tiny bathroom. The sink counter and linoleum floor were both covered in various cleaning supplies and beauty products and count-less unwrapped bars of soap, pieces gouged from their cragged surface like cheddar over a rusted cheese grater. She was lying inside the bathtub, naked, but there was no water. The scissors were in her hand.

And the watchful demon was back.

Except now it wasn't some diametric presence to that of American Christianity's white Jesus. Now it *was* American Christianity, come to condemn Jack for her sexuality, for something she'd never had control of her entire life, something that had confused her. As a child, she'd watched endless movies with heroines who looked like her—pretty, white, feminine, Hollywood's idea of the ideal woman . . . and yet they were never confused about who to fall in love with. They always managed to choose someone her parents would approve of, some classically handsome man with a nine-to-five and weekend drinking buddies. They never turned as another woman passed, a side character or movie set extra. They never questioned themselves.

So why did she?

Why do you? seemed to echo in the demon's guttural chuckle, this Cardigan Man leering down at her naked body in the bathtub.

Why did she *what?*

"Why do I love Ash?"

The Cardigan Man didn't reply, but his widening grin seemed to say, *Yes, yes, why?* even though that was a ridic-ulous thing—he was wearing a gasmask, she couldn't even *see* his grin, could she? It should be impossible for that grin to stretch past the mouthpiece and further still, past the buckles . . .

Her eyes swept back down to the object in her hand. Scissors.

She dropped them. She winced at the sound they made on the linoleum.

"I love Ashley because she's *there* for me."

The Cardigan Man stayed silent, and yet she saw it in his eyes: *She is? There for you?*

"Yes, of course she is, she's always—"

But those eyes hovering above the gasmask suggested otherwise. *She was there to stop me, was she?*

No.

Her wife hadn't been there for that.

She hadn't stopped him from punching Jack, twice, at the river.

She hadn't believed Jack when she saw him by the laundry.

And she hadn't been there on Friday the 13th.

Hadn't been there to stop the Cardigan Man . . .

To stop me from infecting you, his eyes said. His sick, hacking laughter agreed.

Jack crossed her arms over her chest. At his words she'd felt her nipples harden. Goosebumps had plucked up her arms, too, but she didn't want *him* thinking she liked this. Her cheeks flushed in shame. Just her body letting her down again.

"Ash *is* there for me," she whispered. "She . . . she's feeding me, she's paying our bills—"

She's controlling you, is what you mean, the eyes said.

"She—she . . . *no,* that's not what I mean. You don't fucking know what I fucking mean. She's *there* for me. She *is.*"

The eyes said nothing.

"She's just . . ." A realization struck. The grocery store. The Cardigan Man's coughing attack. "She's protecting us. She's quarantining us from each other, in case—in case *she*—"

In case you . . . in case you're sick.

She looked up at him, still hugging her naked body. She began to shiver.

But there's no "in case" about it, Jackie boy . . .

He leaned over the tub, and the gasmask unbuckled at one side and swung down, revealing his impossibly wide grin, and yes, it *was* wide, so wide it split his face in half.

I spat the coronavirus germs, millions of those squirming viral maggots, right down your throat. By now they've swam inside you like a water park ride. Can't you feel the tingle? Feel those little buggers tickling your esophagus and all through your lungs?

She sank her body down to the bottom of the tub, sliding her back until her shoulders dipped below the tub's rim. But still she could see him. See that swinging gasmask like a pendulum, swinging in time with the *tick-tock* of a clock counting down her infection. *Tick-tock, tick-tock—*

Dun dun . . . dun dun . . . dun dun dun dun dun-dun-dun-dun—

The music of *Jaws* echoed out of the tub's drain, as if Pennywise the Clown was crooning the simple melody up from his lair in the sewers of this diseased town. Jack felt the sudden urge to drown it, to drown whatever alien thing was in there. She lunged forward and spun the faucet's hot water on full blast, finally filling the tub and slowly submerging her naked body in steaming water.

A memory came to her of her father, standing

uncomfortably close behind her as he taught her how to wash the dishes. His voice in her ear, telling her that scalding water was good because it killed the germs. That's what she was doing now—she was killing germs. Killing the virus.

The gooseflesh disappeared as quickly as it had arrived—

—and so did the Cardigan Man.

He was gone. The singing voice had drowned and gone away, too, and the water felt scalding hot but she was afraid to stop it lest the demon come back, so she let the water stream out and over her. She sank into its depths; the water was so hot it prickled her eyelids and she briefly worried it would boil her eyeballs like Easter eggs.

She wanted desperately to fling herself from the water, to scramble out of the bathroom and suck in cooler air. But for the first time in what felt like an infinite time loop she felt *free*—or maybe not free but like she was finally escaping whatever had clawed itself inside her. She was killing the germs, just like Daddy taught her. She was burning the poison from her body, purging the toxic waste, cleansing herself of the sin.

She only turned off the faucet when the water was nearly level with the tub's lip. Jack had to move slowly as she turned it off, to avoid slopping water onto the bathroom floor. Once she'd settled back down in the water, she realized she had unconsciously crossed her arms across her chest, protecting herself again.

But the Cardigan Man was gone.

She uncrossed her arms slowly, calming herself. She lay in the warmth for some time, just breathing. She felt safe again. Alone.

Jack pressed her palms against her chest, feeling her slow heartbeat. She slid her fingers, tingling in the underwater warmth, across her breasts and down her belly. Once she hit that patch of fluttery skin beneath her belly button, she moaned and smiled at the butterfly sensation it gave her. Ash liked to tickle that part of her belly, the band of skin just above the line of her panties. Jack would giggle and squeal and squirm and then she'd have to tackle Ash to make it stop.

She closed her eyes, thinking of Ash. Her wife . . . her love. Marrying Ash had banished that shameful fear of her sexuality: to swear her devotion to not a man or a woman but to a person, *her* person. And she wasn't going to let her imagination conjure up some bigoted asshole like the Cardigan Man to make her doubt herself or her wife. Her body was her own.

She moaned pleasurably, feeling her fingers slide further down her body, and gave in to the sensation of sliding first one and then two fingers down and inside of the folds of her vagina.

"Mmmm . . ."

After some time, as meaningless as the time-looped nightmares, Jack came, relaxed her body entirely, and let the steaming water take her down to sleep.

WHEN SHE WOKE the water was cold. There were more goosebumps now than ever, pebbling across her entire body like braille. She looked down. Her skin was shriveled and pruny.

She didn't know how long she'd been asleep, but she

did know one thing: she hadn't felt such peace as she felt now in . . . she couldn't remember how long. She felt cleansed. She felt healthy. She felt certain the demon was done stalking her. Felt certain she would dry off and step out into the hall and find Ash with her arms spread wide.

She unplugged the tub and climbed out as it drained. A towel hung from the rack by the door, and she grabbed it and sat on the toilet's closed lid as she dried off. As she toweled the cold drips of water from her skin and her gooseflesh disappeared, her sense of peace only grew.

She smiled.

The last part of her body to dry off was her calves and feet. She hummed as she bent over her legs—she didn't know what, but it sure as hell wasn't the *Jaws* theme. Her calves dried, she sat straight again and lifted her left foot, crossing her calf over her other knee. She covered her foot with the dry end of the towel and pressed against it, hugging her foot with the fluffy fabric—first her toes, then the inside arch of her foot, then her heel.

There was a strange springiness under the towel. Under her hands.

A spike of heat shot through her, dispersing the last of the goosebumps. But this was of a different breed from the warmth of peace cocooning her—a cocoon of peace that had just cracked open and sloughed off of her far too soon.

She felt the skin of her foot through the cotton, still unwilling to lift the towel and peek at what lay beneath. Applying pressure didn't hurt, so that was good . . . but it also didn't feel normal. What should be the hard ridge of her heel seemed . . . *pliable* somehow. Her fingers sunk into flesh that yielded and gave, molding around the pressure like some kind of thick balloon.

She held her breath as she lifted the towel away.

At first what she saw confused her. Her foot appeared the same, but it was as if she were looking at it through a warped lens—like it was not her foot but its reflection in a funhouse mirror. She inched the fingers of one hand to that spot along the hard, curved edge of her heel, that spot where reality seemed to have dripped like Dali . . . but her fingers stayed resolutely the same. It wasn't her eyesight that was sullied, but the flesh of the heel itself.

The flesh had bubbled out along the outline of the heel, maybe a four-inch crescent of skin. It wasn't discolored or paining her in any way. What was it? A blister?

A parasite, whispered a voice from the bathtub drain.

"Shut up," she told it, but her own voice came out shaky.

Ash would know what this was. In fact, she was constantly nagging Jack to moisturize her feet—this must be related to that. Her wife would give her the necessary "I told you so" and then a moisturizing regimen and the swelling (if that's what this was) would go down in no time.

She finished drying the rest of the foot with the towel and switched legs, setting her right foot on her other knee so she could dry it. But she froze before she could cover this foot with the towel.

And she screamed.

* * *

THE SECOND TIME SHE SCREAMED, it wasn't because of what she saw on her foot. It was because someone burst into the bathroom through the pocket door that led to the walk-in closet, which had been slightly ajar. In her panic, she saw it all in a flash of prescience: the Cardigan Man lunging into the bathroom, not with a gasmask or rotting flesh or even a cardigan, but looking perfectly healthy, because this was the *real* Cardigan Man, come to finish the job. He'd broken in while Jack was asleep in the bathwater, and he'd beaten Ashley unconscious and raped her and killed her and the whole time Jack had been taking a fucking bath just one thin wall away. She'd *let* it happen, and now her wife's bloody and desecrated body lay discarded on the floor and he was coming in here to finish Jack off—

"Jack, what is it? Are you okay?"

But it wasn't the Cardigan Man. Of course.

It was Ash. Not beaten or bloodied and still very much alive and obviously concerned because Jack had just screamed bloody murder over her foot.

Her *foot.*

She looked down, for an instant certain that this would turn out to be a hallucination, too, and that there was nothing wrong with her fucking foot—

She screamed again.

"Jack, please, what *is* it?"

She looked back up at Ash, still standing there, uncertain.

She whispered: "My foot."

"Your . . . ?" Ash looked at the foot Jack still had propped on her knee.

Jack whispered, "My *foot*, it's—"

"Oh my *god*, what *happened?*"

Ash rushed to her and dropped to her knees, hovering her hands over Jack's foot but halting, afraid to touch it. They both stared down at it in shock.

Jack's right foot looked as though maybe it had once held the same mysterious stretch of raised and bubbled skin as her other foot. But then it had grown from there, like an alien blob in a '50s horror film. It looked now like a tumor of glistening skin had sucked itself over Jack's entire heel and was now climbing to subsume her inside ankle as well. The tight bulbous skin of the growth (if that's what this was) was not entirely opaque: a semi-translucence the milky yellow color of pus, shiny yet splotchy, like dead skin stretched to its ripping point.

"How did this . . . ?"

Ash's question trailed off as they both stared down at the monstrosity. Right before their eyes, it seemed to almost imperceptibly expand . . . to swell out . . . the untainted skin just beneath the ankle bone retreating as the tumor climbed.

With it climbed Jack's sense of insurmountable dread.

Ash's hovering hands finally broke their spell and descended over the foot—

"Don't touch it!"

Ash froze, looking up at Jack in alarm.

Jack tried to swallow down her fear so she could speak. "I just—" She swallowed again. It felt as though stones were clogging her throat. "I was just in the tub, taking a bath, and I fell asleep, and . . . and I mean I don't know what this *is* but it was here when I got out of the tub to dry myself and it's starting on my other heel, too, I think—"

"Here, let me see." Ash didn't touch Jack's foot, but she motioned for her to show her the left one. When Jack switched legs so her left foot was up on her knee, Ash did touch her, but it was with careful fingers on either side of the raised skin. She finally nodded. "Not nearly as bad, but it does look like it might be the same thing."

The same parasite, the Cardigan Man's voice said from the drain.

"*What* thing, though?" Jack asked her wife, ignoring the voice from the drain. "What could have caused this? I was just . . ." Her voice grew thick with tears. "Just taking a bath."

Ash stood, taking the towel from Jack's hands and draping it over her shoulders, and Jack realized she was still naked. She had never felt so unsexy in her life.

"Come here, baby, let's get you in bed. I'll google it," Ash said.

As Ash helped her hobble into the hallway and to the bedroom (a less cramped path to the bed than through the walk-in), Jack tried and failed to ignore the chuckling voice that dripped from the drained tub:

You've gone parasitic, Jackie boy.

AFTER JACK HAD CALMED DOWN, sipping her tea and propped against pillows so that her feet could be elevated above the surface of the bed, Ash grabbed her laptop and got to work solving the mystery of her wife's monster feet.

"Was the water hot, baby?"

Jack nodded hesitantly. "Not, like, *boiling.* I was inside the tub when I filled it, so I didn't have to, like, work my body into the water by degrees. It was comfortable."

Ash's eyes skimmed the computer screen in the bedroom's dimness. "How long were you in the water?"

"I don't know."

Ash looked at her over her laptop. "A few minutes? An hour?"

"I don't *know* . . . I think I fell asleep. So a while?"

Ash nodded. "Judging by your pruning skin, I'd say a while at least."

Jack sighed, lowering her tea. "But what does that matter? And why are you *smiling*?"

Ash's smile only widened, which just frustrated Jack more, but then her words deflated the tension: "I just . . . I missed hearing your voice."

There was an awkward silence, then Ash pressed on:

"It might matter because, if the water was super hot and you were in there for a while, you may have . . . boiled your skin."

"What, like a lobster?"

Ash giggled. "Yeah, like a sexy, delicious lobster. And, I mean, I can't really find anything to confirm this, but I think . . . maybe calluses or thicker skin is more likely to build pressure or something? A heat blister is all."

Jack heard all this, but she couldn't accept it. She stared at her feet, propped up awkwardly, those sickly sacs of tumorous pus hanging at her heels. This wasn't something as benign as a blister. This was malevolent. This was evil. She knew what this really was.

That time-looped nightmare flashed in her mind.

The Cardigan Man.

His hands holding her against the building.

His mouth coughing on her.

This was the virus.
Jacqueline was sick.

9

ASHLEY &
JACQUELINE

"I'm not a doctor. But I'm, like, a person that
has a good . . . you-know-what."
—President Donald J. Trump

"We here at [Lakeview Homes] understand that
our tenants may have been affected by the current nationwide situation, but we would like to
remind said tenants that they are not the only
ones affected. That is why, effective immediately, all late rent penalties have been upgraded
to eviction notice. To ensure you remain with
us here at [Lakeview], please pay all rent and
utilities in full and on time."
—a sample of the mass letters
emailed out to renters across the U.S.

ASH WOKE TO SCREAMING. Her first early-morning
thought was:
That can't be Jack.

Jack lay next to her, still sound asleep. Almost two weeks had passed since the bathtub incident; Jack's heels were still bubbling like something out of a Cronenberg movie, but their dynamic together had taken a dramatic turn for the better. First, Jack had finally become responsive and seemed to have pulled herself out of her perpetual catatonic state; then, amazingly, Jack had asked Ash to stay the night in their bed with her instead of out on the couch like she'd done the last month.

The screaming continued.

Ash tiptoed out of the bedroom and clicked the door shut. It was a miracle that this racket hadn't woken Jack, as her sleep was typically troubled and scattershot, but Ash would take any miracle she could get. She swept silently through the hall and to the front door to get a clearer earshot of the commotion.

The screaming raged on, and now that it had come somewhat into focus for Ash, a chill ran up her spine. It was clearly a man, though it was hard to tell where he was: outside? in a nearby apartment? It sounded as though the man were having a mental breakdown. Violent smashing noises punctuated his screams. His voice was guttural and panicked and spewed out a continuous stream of profanities and rantings against someone. Ash couldn't quite make out the words.

It was the most violent shouting Ash had ever heard.

This was a strange feeling, hearing actual noise from other people nearby. Ash had grown used to the silence. Although everyone was supposedly home and shut inside 24/7 against the pandemic, daily noises had fallen away. No piano and vocal scales from John, no mechanical work from one of their downstairs neighbors who kept his motorcycle just outside his sliding-glass door, no chanting from the coven of witches at the end of the building, which had usually been a Friday-night tradition. Even downstairs Melanie's hammering had slackened.

A thought struck her: What if this shouting man was Melanie's boyfriend? Ash had only met her a few times, but their downstairs neighbor seemed sweet, just a quiet young woman (quiet except for that hammer) who used to have her boyfriend over before the pandemic and have loud sex in the middle of the night (okay, maybe Melanie wasn't quiet at all). What if this was her boyfriend, breaking the stay-at-home order to come break up with his girlfriend? Ash had read how relationships were ending at a much faster rate during this pandemic. In China, something like four hundred married couples had filed for divorce as soon as the quarantine order was lifted.

If that were true, it sounded like the breakup wasn't going well.

In fact, it sounded to Ash like this guy was mere seconds away from committing murder.

What should I do? Call the police?

The police would be too late. Whatever this guy was working himself up to, he was moments away from exploding.

Before she could talk herself out of it, Ash opened the coat closet, fished out a scarf to wrap around her mouth and nose, took out the broom, and unscrewed the long metal handle from the bristle base.

With her makeshift weapon firmly in her grip, she unlocked the front door and hinged it open a few inches, cringing at the creaking sound that might wake up Jack. What would she say if she found out Ash was going outside again?

She stopped. She knew what she'd say. Jack would say Ash was selfish. She'd go right back into Paranoia Land and say Ash was trying to kill them, was trying to let in her fucking Cardigan Man to finish the job.

Just open the door, Ash. She'll never know.

But she didn't. She couldn't. Not after all the progress they'd made together. So Ash just stood there, inches from the outside world, holding her useless makeshift weapon and listening.

It was clear now that the yelling wasn't coming from directly downstairs after all. And it seemed to be winding down. Another man's voice had joined it; someone had had the same thought as Ash and come to investigate, done what Ash was too cowardly to do lest Jack have another freak-out. Now he was maybe half a dozen doors down, trying to calm the shouting guy. Ash caught a snatch of the guy's explanation of why he'd flipped his shit, and it all came clear.

"It's Doug, fucking *Doug*! That fucking piece of shit emailed me a fucking *eviction* notice this morning, for fucking NOTHING. Says he's tired of my fucking *NEIGHBORS*"—this part he said very loudly, as though making sure the offending neighbor heard the accusation—"emailing him about the noise I make when I'm working on my projects. *WHAT THE FUCK AM I SUPPOSED TO DO, WHERE THE FUCK AM I SUPPOSED TO LIVE NOW, THE STATE IS FUCKING SHUT DOWN, I'M GONNA FUCKING MURDER THAT FUCKING SON OF A BITCH—*"

More entreaties from the Good Samaritan neighbor, and the guy seemed to calm down.

Ash quietly returned the handle and scarf to the closet, berating herself for not having a spine. What if the guy *had* been just beneath them, beating Melanie to death? Would Ash really have just left one woman to her fate so as to not incur the wrath of another?

She shook her head. It didn't matter, anyway—it wasn't a murderous boyfriend, it was a man learning he had nowhere to go during a pandemic. She closed the closet door and put on coffee in the kitchen. She listened, but the shouting seemed to have ended for good.

Doug. Fucking Doug. Ash had learned from the start that their landlord was an uptight rich asshole who wanted nothing more than to not hear jack shit from his residents and make his living with minimal effort. And yet the dude was constantly sending mass emails threatening to tow cars he didn't recognize or threatening eviction to anyone seen smoking on the premises or any number of things. Ash had always thought the guy was all bark and no bite.

Apparently not.

An eviction stay had been issued in this county almost immediately after the shit hit the fan. Companies were going out of business too fast to count, unemployment was skyrocketing, and people were panicking about how they were going to pay their rent or mortgage or land tax.

But today was the first day of May. Ash remembered vaguely seeing something about the eviction moratorium not being extended past April. Doug must have seen that same report and jumped at the chance.

"Jesus H. Christ," Ash muttered.

She poured the percolated coffee—black and bitter, the creamer having long since run out—but paused on her way out of the kitchen. There was the pantry, staring at her, taunting her. Like the screaming wasn't coming from outside, from her neighbor; it was coming from inside the empty void of the pantry, screaming at her to fill it. There was a monster in the pantry and it was called starvation.

She'd blown her last chance of grocery shopping back on that first day, March 13th, at H-E-B, spent all that time driving there and all that effort finding food and helping that stranger and running from crazy racists, only to leave that food on the floor, unpaid for and useless to her and Jack. She'd jumped on her computer at midnight every night since, the time when H-E-B was supposedly opening up new windows for delivery, and every midnight the delivery windows would fill up before she could even click on a time. A few nights her order had gone through, only to either get canceled later or just disappear or be ignored.

Before quarantine, Ash and Jack went grocery shopping every couple of weeks. They had a small kitchen, so there really wasn't enough space for a full month's supply. Luckily they'd *just* gone shopping a couple days before everything hit critical—or rather, *Ash* had gone shopping, and Jack had stayed inside in case the cardigan-wearing boogeyman lay in waiting (but that wasn't fair, Ash scolded herself—it turned out the boogeyman *had* been out there, and Jack had been right). Ash had managed to stretch those usually two weeks' worth of food across just over seven weeks; it helped that Jack barely ate, but things had reached "totally fucked" at this point.

The pantry was essentially empty.

There had been several strikes from the workers for

apps like Instacart protesting about working in such un-safe conditions, and Ash had been leery of hiring some outsourced rando who wasn't following the same health and safety measures as H-E-B, but this was turning des-perate. She couldn't live on coffee grounds and oatmeal forever. She'd have to bite the bullet and figure out some kind of quick delivery of essential foods she could stretch across many meals. Rice, quinoa, *something*. And she'd have to make sure the delivery happened while Jack was asleep. Maybe she could give instructions to leave the food outside without knocking, and she could nip out to grab it during one of Jack's seemingly endless naps. Yes, she was talking again, had invited Ash back to their bed-room, but Ash was kidding herself if she thought the Car-digan Man problems had just gone away.

Ash sighed. *Oh, Jack . . .*

She sipped her coffee and went to make the Instacart order. That done, she stared at their own growing stack of bills—not to mention the urgent mass emails from Doug reminding all tenants that rent was due REGARD-LESS OF WORLD EVENTS—and she wondered . . .

Ash wondered when it would be Jack out there, breaking shit and screaming about murdering their landlord.

JACK WOKE TO THE SMELL of coffee.

These were her favorite mornings—soft light peeking through the blinds, birdsong flitting in the silent distance, and coffee brewed to a potency only Ash could acquire, so that its smell permeated every corner of their apart-ment. Coffee itself was too acidic for Jack, and often made her feel sick if she drank more than a small cup, but its smell . . . that smell was home.

She sat up—and then reality returned.

Her feet. Boils climbed her heels like a slow-growing fungus.

The right one in particular kept Jack in a constant state of panic during her waking hours. It had grown to encompass her entire ankle as well, and its sickly yellow skin was so shiny and tight she was sure it would pop any day now. But what would emerge when it did?

Another growing certainty had pulled Jack's nerves taut.

That she was sick.

This wasn't a certainty borne out of her time-looping hallucinations, either. Now she had tangible *proof* of what the Cardigan Man had done to her. It may have taken weeks for his coughed-up contagion to travel through her entire system, down the miles and miles of veins that made up her body's circuitry, but now it had manifested on her feet. Under her skin. The virus had searched for a chink in Jack's armor from the inside, and her falling asleep in that steaming bath had been the opportunity it needed to erupt forth from its host like a Chest Burster in *Alien* (another movie Ash had made her watch).

The rational part of Jack's mind—a small part, but still there—reminded her that this pandemic's virus only took one or two weeks to manifest, not *six* . . . but, the rest of her argued, this was a disease we still knew very little about. It mutated faster than scientists could track, and besides, weren't there always outliers? She was an outlier—of course she was—and her body had bucked the virus particularly hard but not hard enough and it had finally poked its little squirming head out and breathed her in deep.

Jack shook this thought away, breathing in deep herself. Ground coffee beans. It was that coffee smell, that *everything is fine and the world is at peace* scent, that finally tipped her feeling of unreality into a calm reserve. She would act. She wouldn't let the Cardigan Man drag her back into that hellish nightmare scape she'd spent the last however-long spiraling down into. One simple action, that's all it would take to claw herself from the maw of Alice's rabbit hole and out of Fucked-Up Wonderland.

Not wanting Ash to know she was awake just yet, Jack climbed from bed and tiptoed to the walk-in closet. Having boils that extended beneath one's heels made walking a bit of a balancing act. She felt like some mythical satyr walking on the fore of its hind legs, a genderbent, bisexual Mr. Tumnus returning to the land of Narnia.

Through the walk-in closet she emerged into the bathroom and quickly stepped across the linoleum and closed the door leading to the hallway. That fresh scent of coffee washed over her anew, strengthening her resolve.

She turned to the sink and found what she needed. A safety pin. Scissors. The first-aid kit full of gauze, antibacterial cream, and bandages. Supplies in hand, she balanced herself and sat on the closed toilet seat.

Two separate flashes of *déjà vu* hit her at the same time, making her vision momentarily spotty:

Sitting on this same toilet seat, skin wrinkly from a calming bath, drying herself with a warm, fluffy towel, mere moments away from discovering something alien growing from her feet—

Standing in front of the mirror in her childhood bathroom, holding scissors poised over her bared wrist, willing herself to do it, to get it over with—

She shook her head, steadying her vision. *Coffee,* she thought, breathing in. *A normal life with my loving wife. That's what I want. Prove it to Ash, Jackie boy—*

She scolded herself for using that nickname, shot the bathtub drain a look, as if daring it to tell her she couldn't do this, daring it to sing. Then she placed the supplies on the floor and got to work.

She would ease herself into it with the smaller of the boils. She lifted her left foot to her knee, brandished the unclasped safety pin, took a deep breath through her nose, and stabbed into the center mass of the bubbled skin.

It didn't yield as much as she'd expected, yet she didn't feel the tip of the pin as she pushed it harder into her heel. Finally, with a reluctant *psssst!*, the boil began a slow deflation as a thick yellow liquid escaped from the hole around the puncturing pin.

"Shit, shit, shit, *shit,*" she hissed.

With her other hand she yanked a long strip of toilet paper from the roll and dumped it on the bathroom floor beneath her. It caught the blister's discharge before it could smear on the linoleum.

Then, still with her other hand, she began to press and massage around the pin. A part of her was fascinated with this; it was almost an out-of-body experience, watching herself dispassionately poke holes in her own person and extract the unwanted toxin like some mad scientist experimenting on themself. She had never been squeamish, but still: the idea of dealing with this on her own, without Ash here to do it all, or even help, seemed almost laughable.

"But I'm *doing* it," she whispered. She shot another

glare at the bath drain. "Suck my dick, Cardigan Man."

The draining and dressing of the first boil went fairly well, fast and painless. She was holding out hope that the skin of the boil would mend back into her heel, because the idea of hacking through her own thick skin with scissors threatened to shatter her current sense of calm.

One foot down, she switched it with her right one.

Her calm shattered.

So far, she had avoided watching this foot's descent into some kind of prosthetic special effect for *The Thing*; looking at it now brought a small, wordless moan out of her gut, like air being let out of a helium balloon. The boil had grown beyond comprehension. How far could skin stretch until it exploded? Hers extended like a hideous beach ball, with her heel sucked into its middle, a murky shadow in its digestive tract. The bulbous skin was stretched past recognition, an oily, tight surface almost entirely translucent. The thing wobbled like a water balloon, so full it was of pus—of that alien sludge of Jack's nightmares.

No.

Of the Cardigan Man's diseased saliva.

No . . .

Bile shot up Jack's throat, but she forced it down.

No!

Taking up the safety pin again, before she could completely lose her nerve and bring Ash rushing into the bathroom with her screams, Jack squinted at the mass hanging from her foot and brought the sharp point down.

It wasn't the loud *pop!* and *gush!* she'd been expecting. She supposed that was a good thing—she hadn't put down nearly enough toilet paper, it would have drenched the bathroom floor in a wave of sickly whatever-the-fuck-this-was—but a part of her wished it had . . . wished it was over and done with. Part of her wanted to take the scissors and saw off the whole goddamn foot. Maybe the entire leg. Get one of those badass prosthetics you see amputee surfers with after a shark attack. Hell, she could design her own prosthetic with a detachable dildo—Ash would love that. Sell some in her Etsy shop.

Jack giggled in her horror and slapped a hand over her mouth.

Don't lose it now. You can do this.

Moving quickly once more, she laid down several more layers of toilet paper, said "Fuck it" and laid down a hand towel too. Then she got to work methodically squeezing the pus out of her like toothpaste. Again, she didn't feel it, though her horror had risen to be a palpable chalky taste on her tongue. She smelled shit and realized it was her own bad breath, held it, turned to the door to get a scant whiff of that morning coffee. Draining this second, monstrous boil (if that's what this was) took much longer, and Jack actually felt sweat pour out of her as she worked.

When she got down to the actual meat of her foot, the pain finally arrived. To squeeze the last of the pus from the widening hole in the boil sac, she was pressing against her shin bone. A sharp *ting!* sang up through her bones like a tuning fork. She clamped down on her bottom lip to stifle any crying out. Bit down harder. Drew blood.

And then it was done.

That part, at least.

She was panting from the exertion, from tamping

down the pain, when she realized what came next.

"Oh, fuck," she muttered.

The scissors.

There would be no leaving this deflated skin intact, hoping it would graft itself back into the body of the foot. Without the liquid to fill it, the thing was a huge mass of slippery, thin folds of skin. It resembled a flappy bat's wing the color of a naked mole-rat. If she didn't cut it away from her foot, it would tear eventually, and potentially take healthy skin with it and make the wound bleed even more than it already was now.

And so she cut it away with the scissors, trying (and failing) not to think about those waking nightmares of her bringing the scissor teeth to her wrist or holding the scissors in the bathtub or using them to saw the wriggling slug that once was her tongue from her mouth. She cut as carefully and neatly as she could, the most important arts-and-crafts project of her life, and yet still the pain made spots dance in her vision. At one point the scissors slipped and the tip of one blade dipped into the bloody center of the wound and it felt like her whole body had been alchemically transmuted into a Jacqueline-shaped zinc statue and shoved into God's electric socket, filling her with enough electricity to run Austin for a month. But somehow she managed to clamp down on her delirious whimper and choke down a helpless sob.

And she had done it all without Ash.

That done, she stood momentarily, precariously on the balls of her feet, so she could flip up the toilet seat and flush the hated boil sac down the toilet like a used condom.

Flush.

"Jack? You awake?"

Shit. So much for going unnoticed until this was done.

"Yeah, babe, just a second! Pour me some coffee?" Jack called.

No way was she drinking coffee after this. The moment it hit her tongue she'd hurl.

She tried to move quicker now. She applied the antibacterial cream to the wide exposed part of the wound, a huge section of her foot and ankle that now looked like a skinned animal; then she wiped it all away, seeing how it had just mixed with a fresh well of blood, biting her lip the whole time, and reapplied the cream. She positioned two layers of nonstick gauze strips over it (thank Jesus they had nonstick; she couldn't imagine ripping that many bandages from such a deep wound) and wrapped it with two full ACE bandages. Seeing that blood had already begun to spot the bandage on her other foot, she wrapped that one again, too. Finally Jack stood, looked at her pale face in the mirror, and composed herself before walking delicately out into the living room.

"Good morning, baby! Are you . . . how are you feeling?"

The hesitation in Ash's voice didn't surprise her. Even though Jack had begun speaking again after the bath incident, she still hadn't stepped out of the safety of her bedroom, especially since she had basically been bedridden all week—for practical reasons this time, not just because she was a heaping mess of paranoia.

"Oh my god, your *feet!*"

Ash rushed forward and helped Jack over to the couch. Neither of them spoke until they'd successfully propped her feet up with enough pillows that gravity didn't bring her bandaged heels down to touch any surfaces.

"Did something happen, baby? Why didn't you call for help?"

"I . . ."

Jack paused. It had seemed so important that she did this on her own. But now . . . why *hadn't* she asked Ash for help? Even just to be a presence in the bathroom while she worked, someone to step in if an errant slip of the scissors opened an artery and she bled out on the bathroom floor.

"I didn't want you to have to worry," she finished lamely.

"Oh, baby, you didn't have to do that, I would have—"

"I'm the idiot who did this to herself," Jack cut in, a little more forcefully than she had intended. She was suddenly angry at herself, angry at Ash, but *why*? Ash hadn't done anything to deserve this. To deserve *her*. "I'm the fucking idiot who fell asleep in a boiling pot of water. I—"

She saw the look in Ash's eyes, the look of helpless disapproval, and suddenly remembered why she'd done it by herself. Jack had wanted to show Ash she could help herself, wanted to do this for Ash, for the both of them. In some subtle, vital way, she'd seen this dressing of her wounds as a watershed moment, a turning point, in their marriage. But getting angry at herself now, after finally emerging into the living room, wasn't helping. She wanted to make Ash laugh, make her forget the bad feelings.

"I'm the one who lobstered her own feet."

And it worked: that infectious laughter bubbled up out of Ash's suddenly smiling, cute little face, and Jack giggled, too, and it was genuine.

After a small pause, Ash said, her eyes searching Jack's hesitantly, "How does it feel to be out here again?"

Jack looked at the sunlight streaming through their view out onto a beautiful, nature-filled world, and said, "It feels nice." And she meant it.

Ash beamed. "Let me go get your coffee. We could watch something, snuggle together."

"Sounds perfect."

"Oh, and you won't *believe* what fucking Doug did this morning. Lemme grab the coffee before I spill the tea."

Ash rushed to the kitchen, leaving Jack for a moment.

Jack smiled and thought: *Maybe we'll be okay.*

And this time, the Cardigan Man wasn't there to say otherwise.

10

JACQUELINE & ASHLEY

"The simple fact of science is that we will never create a computer even close to the human brain. That baby's got billions of neurons and trillions of electric pulses and to be honest I'm not even smart enough to explain the computing abilities of my own brain past this sentence. But one thing we humans don't like to talk about is how that amazing super computer in our heads also manages to store the negative. Trauma specifically literally changes your brain's functioning ability. It leaves physical imprints and jars our memory stores. With each unprocessed traumatic experience, the risk of both mental and physical health problems increases. I'll back all these doomsayer proclamations with actual scientific evidence throughout the rest of this article, but here's the TL;DR: trauma is like a virus, and if we let it, it will eat away at us and send us gibbering to the grave."

—"Unprocessed Trauma Will Kill You"
article on medium.com

THEY CAME IN THE NIGHT.

Before, Jacqueline woke from a dreamless sleep. She still felt that lingering sense that things would be all right. She still felt a calm reserve. She felt a sense of victory over her feet today; over her body. Best of all, she felt no trace of the Cardigan Man.

A soft sound came to her from the dark. It was . . . crying. Ash was nestled in the comforter next to her, crying. Her sniffles and whimpers were soft, but they had been just enough to pull Jack from sleep.

Jack didn't have to sit up to look for Ash. With her heels now bandaged, still bleeding and raw from her self-performed surgery, she had been sleeping propped up, her feet elevated and hanging over a stack of pillows, with her back made comfortable against the headboard with enough pillows and blankets to approximate the shape of a hospital bed. She had been afraid of turning over on her side or moving her feet in her sleep, so Ash had jumped at the opportunity to help and gently plumped the bedding around and beneath her.

As her eyes adjusted to the darkness, she saw Ash's huddled form shudder.

"Ash . . . ?"

Ash jerked in surprise. Her face appeared among the blankets, a pale moon in the dark, streaked with two shimmery trails of tears. She sat up, sniffing, and wiped her nose against an arm. "Sorry, b-babe, did I wake you?"

It was an almost physical effort not to stare at the spot where Ash had rubbed her nose. Jack pushed the thoughts from her head—the snot, the mucus, the germs, the virus an invisible respiratory thief in the night—and said, dumbly, "You're crying."

Ash laughed deprecatingly, her voice thick. "Wonders never cease." She sniffed again, wiped her nose and her face, laughed again.

Don't fixate on the germs, Jack told herself. *Fixate on your wife.*

The truth was, part of Jack's new sense of calm was the idea that she wasn't sick after all. She had burst and cut away the boils, and that's all they'd been—boils. No eldritch creature had emerged from the sac and no cough had stolen over her lungs and no deadly virus had leapt down her throat that day outside. The virus showed itself in seven days, not *weeks,* and its symptoms weren't blisters as big as sin and paranoia to match.

So, she wasn't sick . . . which meant she'd subjected Ash to weeks—no, *months*—of hell for no reason. Simply because she was afraid.

Here Ash was, crying herself to sleep, clearly not okay after weeks and weeks of taking care of a zombie for a wife. Wasn't it the least Jack could do in return to be there for her now?

Before the silence could drag on between them any longer, Jack pushed herself up from her bedding and awkwardly scrambled to her knees. Her bandaged heels successfully facing up instead of pressed into the mattress, she crawled to Ash.

Ash blinked, clearly surprised, but said nothing.

"I love you," Jack whispered.

Ash's face scrunched up. More tears fell.

Jack whispered, "I love you so much."

Sobs escaped, as though Ash were desperately holding her breath.

The patter of a thousand children's feet above them.

Ash's sob turned into a strangled squeak.

Jack smiled, and now, for some reason that escaped her in the moment, she was crying too. "It's just the rain, baby."

As the rain built to a steady white noise all around them, they laughed, tears still falling between them.

Ash wiped her face again and took a deep, shuddering breath. "Babe . . ."

"Yeah?"

The fear stabbed Jack just then. She was suddenly sure that the next words to fall from Ash's lips would be about separation or, worse, the D word, or the dreaded *You need to get help*—

"Can I kiss you?"

Jack stared at Ash's tear-stained face in the dark, surprised by the question. But then . . . *should* she be surprised? Ash was crying after they'd had their first nice afternoon in months, crying because, well, one nice afternoon didn't just make everything better, did it? So maybe Ash *was* having thoughts of separation or divorce or *You need to get help* and the thoughts had made her cry. And here she was asking Jack for a kiss. *Asking.* The only times she'd done that were when she'd jokingly quoted *Jaws*—

"Give us a kiss."

"Why?"

"Because I need it."

—but this wasn't that. This was serious. This was something like desperation.

Years ago, when she and Ash had first made love, Jack was shy. She'd never slept with a woman before, and never had her head been filled with so many questions, so much doubt, as in the hesitating moments before letting

Ash undress her. But Ash had taken control, had whispered that it would be all right, and it had been. In fact, it had been more than all right, it had been *revelatory*. Jack had never experienced her life come into such crystalline focus when they held each other, sweating into each other, and this small, vivacious woman brought her to a climax.

And that had been their dynamic: Jacqueline, the shy yet sensual being, and Ashley, the one who took charge and made the first moves and steered the vehicle of their sexual life. But here things had changed, and Ash was hesitant now, asking "Can I kiss you?" Suddenly Jack knew that if she was going to make any steps toward fixing their marriage, toward mending what she'd broken with her paranoia, with giving herself up to her fear, if she had any chance of doing that, this time it had to be her who made the first move.

She inched forward in the raining dark and kissed her wife.

As their lips met, Ash's eyes stayed open, and Jack, her own eyes open now as she deepened the kiss, saw them widen in surprise, saw tears pour harder, and she knew that she was right. Their marriage was broken. She, Jack, had infected it with her sickness, and if she didn't fix it she'd have to watch it die with the rest of the world.

After her first moments of frozen surprise, Ash seemed to accept Jack's advances, and she softened into the kiss. A few hiccupping sobs, and then her body melted into Jack's. Jack lifted her to her knees, so that they were both kneeling on the mattress like before an altar, and they embraced. Jack's tongue slipped hesitantly into the kiss.

They broke apart, leaning their foreheads against each other, their combined breath drowning out the rain on the roof.

"You're sure about this?" Ash whispered.

"I want you, babe," Jack replied.

"But . . . your feet—"

"Don't worry about me. I'll be careful."

They stayed like that. Breathing into each other.

The rain thickened.

"I love you, too, Jack," Ash whispered.

And then they were together again, kissing, pulling at each other's clothes with an almost heartbreaking desperation. Jack loved the way Ash's petite body felt beneath her hands. Sweaty and flushed with excitement. Like on their wedding night. She kissed her lips, her face; she brushed her lips along the inner curve of her ear. She let Ash's hair tickle her. She was aware, in the dark, of how her own body must feel after all this time. Starvation made her ribs poke out at a sickly angle. She was aware, in the dark, of how Ash's body, on the other hand, felt strong and healthy.

She pushed that thought away and gave herself to Ashley.

All the while their hands moved, explored. Touched the other. Whispered over their skin. Ash cupped Jack's breast and brought it to her mouth and teased the nipple with her teeth and Jack moaned. They whispered nothings to each other and said the other's name and *Jesus* and *God* and *Jacqueline* and *Ashley* and *Oh, baby* . . .

* * *

THEY CAME IN THE NIGHT.

After, Jacqueline gasping, holding Ashley's face in her hands so they could keep eye contact as they rode the wave together, the sounds from outside were just part of the rain, part of their experience. Ash still felt that euphoric numb in her bottom lip that came with every orgasm. She still felt an unbreakable connection to this other heaving body entwined with hers.

A soft sound came to them from the dark. It was . . . hammering?

Melanie?

"What's that noise?" Ash whispered.

"Just the rain, babe—"

"No." Her voice rose above a whisper, shattering their post-coital calm. "That *noise*."

They paused, held their breath.

There, rising just above the rain: a tapping that could be a hammer, voices that could be shouting men, a cacophony that could be the television playing a program about construction workers on the factory floor in big industry.

"Jack—"

"WHAT THE FUCK ARE YOU DOING?!"

Ash jumped. A screaming voice cut through the night, somewhere out there. A neighbor?

The men's voices out in the rain became clearer. They were shouting to each other, not bothering to answer the screamed question.

"WHAT THE FUCK, DOUG, FUCK ARE YOU DOING OUT THERE?!"

A thought sent a shiver of *déjà vu* through Ash: *Fucking Doug . . .*

"Babe, what's . . . ?" Jack's eyes were bright in the

dark. Ash could see the fear and paranoia that had left during their time sweating and kissing and moaning, now returning in her face.

"Stay here." Ash bounded from the bed, leaping over piles of clothes still on the floor, through the hallway to the front door. "What the fuck—"

A screaming metal-on-metal electric sound was coming from right behind their front door.

"HELLO?" Ash shouted.

No one answered, but the screaming electric sound whined on. A power tool?

The door began to judder in its frame.

Not wanting to open it and face whatever this was, she pounded on the inside of the door. "HELLO? WHO IS THAT?"

Shouting outside, all along the walkway it seemed, but no response to Ash's question.

"Babe, what is it?"

Ash jumped at the voice. It was Jack, come careening unsteadily on the balls of her feet, standing naked at the mouth of the hallway. It reminded Ash of her own nakedness.

"I—I don't know, it sounds like . . ." Her mouth hung open, speechless. What did it sound like? Like a fucking horror movie. Like something far scarier than *Jaws*.

I used to hate the water.

I can't imagine why.

"Babe?"

Ash shook herself, focused on Jack's questioning, frightened expression. "Go call nine-one-one!"

Jack nodded and Ash turned back to the door. The

absurdity hit her: of the two of them, it was Jack who she sent to call the police—Jack, whose phone had been discarded and left to run out of battery weeks ago; Jack, who moved like a drunk burn victim. But a part of Ash felt certain that if she left the front door, whatever was making that whining metal-on-metal noise would burst through it. A watched pot and all that.

Was that what was happening? Someone was trying to break in? If that were true, it sounded like this someone was part of a *team* of someones trying to break in all across the complex.

"No service!" Jack's voice called. She must have found Ash's phone.

The dropped calls, of course. "Wi-Fi emergency calling!" Ash called over her shoulder.

Just as the metal-on-metal sound stopped, the door no longer lurching in its frame, Jack's pale face peeked around the hallway. "Babe. Wi-Fi's down."

"Oh, fuck, fuck, *fuck*," Ash said. Something told her just restarting the modem wouldn't bring the Wi-Fi back. "Fucking *Doug*."

Jack blinked at her, the phone slack in her hand. "What?"

"Fucking Doug, our fucking landlord." She realized she never told Jack about the evicted neighbor—she'd started to, had gotten so close, and then chickened out, thinking it would undo all of Jack's progress. She'd never told Jack about the daily emails their landlord had sent about paying rent on time and about the million different ways he was waiting for residents to break their lease so he could bring down the wrath of God upon them. "He—"

A screech of feedback, and an amplified voice cut through all the commotion:

"RESIDENTS OF CREEKSIDE, THIS IS YOUR FORMER BUILDING MANAGER. I WOULD LIKE TO INFORM YOU OF YOUR IMMEDIATE RELEASE FROM YOUR CONTRACT. THE BOARD OF TRUSTEES NO LONGER HOLDS CONTROL OF THIS BUILDING, AND I HAVE DECIDED TO— THIS IS FOR YOUR OWN GOOD, YOU KNOW . . . I'VE DECIDED, FOR PUBLIC SAFETY, TO SHUT YOU INSIDE."

"Shut you inside" . . . ?

The meaning rushed through Ash in a galvanic pump of her veins.

"Help me get the door," she said to Jack.

Jack just stood there, frail and empty, her face drained of color.

Ash threw open the coat closet and grabbed the broom, flipped it, spun the bristled attachment off, and closed the closet door so she could open the front door—

"What are you doing?"

But she couldn't stop to explain to Jack. Doug, fucking Doug, was barricading them *inside* the apartment and abandoning them. The Wi-Fi was off—what else had been shut down? For all they knew, fucking Doug would be killing the building's power and pumping poisonous gas into each apartment, and Jack and Ash would die literally coughing up their lungs even without catching the virus.

She unlocked the door and twisted the knob—

"What are you doing?!"

—but it wouldn't budged.

"Jack, help me with the door!"

"No, no . . ."

"Jack, please, *help* me—"

"THE CARDIGAN MAN IS OUT THERE!"

Oh, for fuck's sake, Ash thought, despairing, and pulled harder, and the door finally wrenched open with a shriek of nails being pulled from their track.

Men's shouting: *"Two B, apartment two B!"*

The door had only given a few inches. Ash put a bare foot up against the frame and jerked the knob. A heavy boot came crashing down onto her ankle and she cried out. Pulling back, she jabbed the end of the broom into the space between the door and its frame and felt it hit someone who gave a satisfying "Ow!"

A loud *BANG!* of gunfire; an explosion just to Ash's right—

A man's voice, probably the owner of the boot: "Don't, dumbass, you'll bust the door more!"

They're shooting at us and I've got a fucking broom handle, Ash thought.

And then the broom was jerked in her grasp. She clung to it, but the metal was slippery in her sweaty hands. She cried out. Just as she was sure her one weapon would be wrenched from her hands and then disappear into the night, she yelled out a wordless "HAAAH!" and clung to the slippery titanium like a life preserver. She felt a surge of triumph as it came free of whoever was on the other side of the tug-of-war, then a yelp of surprise as she stumbled backward, feeling suddenly weightless.

Bodies slammed up against the doorframe and yanked the door closed again.

The broom handle clattered to the carpet at her feet,

now useless.

Another screech of feedback and the booming voice:

"DO NOT ATTEMPT ESCAPE. THERE ARE MEN WITH GUNS WHO WILL NOT HESITATE TO SHOOT. I REPEAT: DO NOT ATTEMPT TO ESCAPE."

Through all this, when Ash had turned away from the door, she found Jack crumpled into a naked puddle on the floor, muttering about the fucking boogeyman.

"The Cardigan Man, he knows . . . he knows, he knows, I was wrong and he knows, it's inside, it's inside, he knows and it's inside and I was wrong and . . ."

From the floor, Jack paused in her mutterings long enough to look up at Ash, both of them shivering and naked and sweaty and scared, and said:

". . . and I kissed you."

The door shuddered again in its frame, making Ash jump. When she turned back to the door, she shielded her eyes, crying out. A *whoomp!* and rush different from the constant rain had come from just outside and now a thin line of red glow danced along the border of the door, limning the front entrance in the occasional spark.

Broomless, naked, her crazy wife ranting on the floor, Ash screamed her frustration at the door. She screamed and jumped forward and screamed and bashed her shoulder into the wood, but the door did not so much as budge. It stayed as if poured in concrete. Still she screamed, slammed into the door, again and again and again. She felt the heat of what they were doing out there, felt the heat of being shut inside, trapped like a lab rat left to die after failed experiments. Sparks fell down on her shoulders like embers in a campfire and she hit the door again and again and screamed her throat raw and felt the last of her control be yanked from her, just inches away on the other side of this single piece of wood and yet impossibly out of her reach.

III

CONSUMES

11

ASHLEY

"I have here a joint statement NBC, CBS, ABC, and my own station, CNN, swearing that we will no longer—and never again, for that matter—televise this administration in any way. We believe that we are acting in the public interest; indeed, that we are actually protecting our viewers, the American people. We believe that *true* patriotism means . . . [throws paper away] No, I'm sorry, but I have to say it. If Bill O'Reilly can say it on live television then I can as well. Fuck you, Mister President. Fuck you very much, from the bottom of my heart."

—Jake Tapper
live on CNN, June 2020

ASH WAS CUTTING off all her hair.

What level of quarantine are you? she'd write in a quippy, female-empowerment Instagram post. *I'm officially at the Shaved My Head Out of Manic Boredom quarantine level. Join me? #FeltCuteMightWigLater*

Or that's what she'd write if Instagram still existed.

For all she knew, all social media platforms had gone the way of telegrams and horse-drawn carriages and fucking polio a month ago. A month ago, when their certifiably crazy landlord—fucking *Doug*—soldered and reinforced whatever barricade he'd erected to shut their only exit from this apartment. No more Instagram, no more laundry (so now she had a handful of quarters and she'd never use them, they were collectors' items like the two-dollar bill and the Indian Head Penny, sell them for a good profit on eBay, oh wait no more internet ha-ha), no more grocery delivery, no more run-ins with the Cardigan Man. No more telling herself she'd make the trip down to the water and ride a canoe to the river someday.

No more control.

She looked at her reflection in the bathroom mirror.

No more control, sure, fine, except today she would take back at least a motherfucking modicum of that control. She could hear all the men in her life asking, "How is shaving your head taking back control?" But they didn't get it; they'd never get it. They'd always be the ones following her around with a sneer and a "You're not gay, honey, you just haven't tried the right dick." Like if they dropped their pants to their ankles and shoved their manly penis into her mouth they'd instantly cure her of her queer delusions, she'd finally be able to quit the carpet and get down with the dick like a *real* woman. Until then, in their eyes, she'd never be a *real* woman.

"Fuck you," she said to the mirror.

The scissors went *snip*.

When she'd first resolved to do this, she'd spent a solid thirty minutes looking for the scissors. She knew she'd need to cut away the long strands of hair before she could talk herself into taking the buzzer to her scalp. They'd bought a fancy buzz trimmer a couple years back when Jack wanted to shave one side of her head but was too nervous to go to a salon for the cut. And you'd *think* they would have more than the one pair of scissors after all the money they'd blown on art supplies for Jack's going-nowhere, never-gonna-happen arts-and-crafts Etsy shop.

But when Ash finally found the scissors—in the bathroom, beneath the sink in the bottom of the first-aid kit, hidden away like a murder weapon—she almost gave up the whole idea then and there. The blades of the scissors were gummed up with some kind of dried gunk. Not blood—at least not most of it—but something that had dried a noxious yellow color and looked like little nodules of fat buildup. Like the scissors had succumbed to quarantine life, too, and were binge eating KFC slop buckets.

She couldn't ask Jack about it—well, she *could*, but what would be the point?—so she washed them as best she could and let the scissors soak overnight in Coca-Cola (the last can of Coke they had, is Pepsi okay?). Fully satisfied, and confident she could buck the memory of that . . . *smell* . . . from her mind, she'd set up a haircut station in the bathroom and got to work.

Watching tresses of her raven-black hair tumble down around her like autumn leaves turned out to be just as therapeutic as she'd hoped. Every *snip* of the scissor was a snip back at the patriarchy telling her she wasn't gay, telling her she didn't *really* like women, telling her that her own marriage was a sham, that she wasn't who she said she was, she wasn't Ash—*snip* . . . *snip* . . . *snip* . . .

Her marriage wasn't a sham. *Snip.*

She did love Jacqueline. *Snip.*

She'd known since she was seven that boys weren't for her. *Snip.*

"No, Dad, I won't go on a blind date with your penis-having coworker."

Snip.

"No, Uncle, I've never kissed a guy and I don't need to try it to know if it's for me."

Snip.

"My marriage isn't 'play-acting.' "

Snip.

"I love Jacqueline."

She paused. The scissors cradled the last lock of hair between their teeth, ready to bite. But suddenly she couldn't look herself in the eye.

"You love Jacqueline," she told her neckline.

She forced eye contact with the reflection of a short-haired, out-of-control Ashley and echoed the words she'd spoken on her wedding day, suddenly feeling childish. Feeling small.

"I *do.*"

She cut the last strand. It fell to the sink in a heap of hair. And now she was crying. She'd had to force out the last word—"I *do*"—to keep her voice from breaking. Why? Because the truth was "I do *not*"?

But she *did.* She'd meant it. Every word of it. Every second of every hour out in the hot sun at both the ceremony and reception, she'd meant every muscle of the smile on her face, every glistening tear she'd shed. She'd never had a happier day than her wedding day.

But what about now?

Could things change so completely in just a few years?

A few months, she amended. It had never been so bad in California. Or maybe it had . . . but, she thought bitterly, it wasn't like she could revisit her journals and find out. She'd stopped writing in those a long time ago.

She wiped the tears from her cheeks with the back of one hand. Strands of cut hair stuck in the salty wetness. With her hair like this, halfway through the cut, tufts sticking out at different lengths, she looked like an escaped mental patient. She looked like—

Like Jack.

No. She couldn't think like that. No matter how much things may have changed. *No matter what*—wasn't that, after all, how they'd both ended their vows?

She wiped her face again, sniffed back the snot.

Take back control.

After a few more *snips*, ignoring her set jaw and trembling chin, Ash threw the scissors in the sink with the discarded hair. As far as she was concerned, those scissors could fall into a black hole and she'd never miss them again. What *was* that shit coated all over the teeth like weeks-old gore? Did Jack use them on herself somehow?

Her feet. That must be it.

Ash shuddered. She refused to think further on it. If Jack had taken scissors to those boils, she was afraid of what might be under those bandages—bandages she hadn't seen Jack change or take off in all the weeks and weeks since. Could an untended wound like that get infected, or . . . ?

No. Ashley needed to focus on herself. Jack might as well be worlds away right now. Ash couldn't reach her if she tried.

Take control, she thought at her reflection.

She took up the trimmer, fully charged, and got to work shedding her head of all those dead skin cells. She was Theseus's ship, rebuilding her own identity over and over. That's all hair was—the skin of the body, pushing its dead self out to be pruned from the healthy, living trunk. You completely regrow your entire body's cell population every seven years—hadn't she learned that in biology class? If so, she was a new person every seven years, and why not today, on her twenty-eighth birthday? A new body, and she was the ship's captain.

Yes. Today she was twenty-eight years old.

Or at least she was pretty sure today was her twenty-eighth birthday. She couldn't really check her phone's calendar anymore.

Happy birthday to me.

Birthdays weren't terribly important to her—she'd learned not to get her hopes up in her teen years, when her parents were still coming to terms with their only daughter having a *girlfriend*—but it was still bizarre to wake up on your birthday and know you were completely isolated. She imagined this might be what many prisoners experienced every year, knew it was ridiculous to feel disappointed by some arbitrary holiday, but still . . . she was married. She was supposed to have another person on her team. Even with everything else, couldn't you always count on your partner to celebrate you? She knew it was selfish of her—not to mention ridiculous, considering there were much more pressing things to feel disappointment about.

Like being cut off from the outside world.

Like having a wounded wife who couldn't seek medical attention—

—and who was in no mental state to even *know* she needed medical attention.

Like being trapped inside this apartment.

No cell reception.

No internet.

Little food.

The first day of being trapped had been spent assessing the level to which they were actually trapped. The front door was shut and solid beyond even budging in its frame. She had no idea what Doug and whatever men he'd corralled had done, but whatever it was had been effective. At first, she'd been terrified to explore other escape options. After all, the men outside had guns and they weren't afraid to use them. During the first month of Texas's stay-at-home orders, she'd read online that gun and ammo stores had been almost entirely cleaned out before being forced to close with the rest of the state. Who knew if these men were among those frenzied buyers—who knew what kind of heavy artillery and endless supply of automatic assault rifles these men at fucking Doug's beck and fucking call had at their disposal?

And then she'd noticed the pantry . . . she vaguely recalled feeling some kind of explosion during the hectic panic at the front door, echoing the *BANG!* of the gun outside. Now she saw that the bullet had slammed into the pantry just inches from her and then through the unopened Instacart delivery of rice and finally lodged itself in the rock wall across the room (not enough to bring the wall down, unfortunately). Ash had squatted down and retrieved every grain of rice from the kitchen and pantry floor while Jack gibbered on the carpet ten feet away. If they were truly trapped, they couldn't waste a single piece of food.

Afterward, she'd explored the apartment wall that held the front entrance. No windows. Those goddamn hippie architecture students. Not a single fucking window of penetrable glass, not in the hallway, not in the kitchen, not even in the bathroom. Though, she supposed Doug's men would have reinforced any windows if they had existed, just like they had with all the doors.

The building was old, and made before the age of contractors cutting corners with cheap materials. Its foundations were solid. None of these walls would give to someone without the proper tools, especially someone as tiny as Ashley, armed only with a pair of grimy scissors and a broom handle. Hell, one of the walls was made of huge slabs of pocked stone, for fuck's sake.

The back wall was the only one with windows, and even then it was just the two: their big "used to be a glass sliding door without a balcony once upon a time" window, and the small window in the bedroom—which, frustratingly, didn't even open. No rusted out-of-use tracks to slide the pane through, just a completely sealed window looking out on an empty creekside that might as well be a whole universe away instead of a fifteen-foot tumble.

Ash had stared out the big sliding-door window for hours at a time over the following days and weeks. She imagined that if she really wanted to, she could find a way to break the glass. She'd already checked to see if she could MacGyver the window into functioning in its original purpose as a sliding door, but it seemed Doug had gotten someone (possibly the same person who shut them inside here) to solder the frame. Its sliding days were over. And even if she could get it open, through sliding or breaking, what then? No way was she jumping that far down. She could throw their mattress down first, but how much cushion would that be against a two-story drop to concrete? If they had a ladder or something they could bridge the gap from the window to the big ash tree and from there climb down to the ground. She could do like they do in the movies and tie together curtains and sheets and whatever and then use it as a rope to climb down, but even *that* seemed dubious.

And besides, any of those options involved one other factor.

Leaving Jack.

No way was Jack in any kind of physical or mental condition to follow along with the kind of chaotic, strenuous getaway plan that their escape would require. And all the crazy schemes Ash had cooked up in her imagination depended on this being a one-way ticket. No coming back. No scaling the building back to the broken window or climbing the tree back to the nonexistent ladder or pulling herself back up the Frankensteined rope of curtains and sheets. So leaving this apartment would mean—

It would mean leaving her wife.

She refused to do that.

Ash looked at herself in the mirror, turning off the electric trimmer.

In the silence, she told her now-shaven reflection:

"I love Jacqueline."

I do.

* * *

THERE WAS ANOTHER REASON they couldn't leave.

But Ash didn't like to think about it.

The reason kept waking her up in the middle of the night. The reason crept up on her and burst into her memory, sounding just as clear and as world-endingly loud in her head as when it had happened. The reason made her cry more than she'd cried in her life.

It had happened just a week after their imprisonment inside the apartment. Ash had exhausted every option of escape she could find, went over them again and again in her mind, and still kept coming back to the one fact that she couldn't leave Jack. But that didn't mean someone *else* couldn't come get them, take away from here—maybe even bring Jack somewhere she could get proper help. Somewhere that could help her get back to the Jack that Ash had fallen in love with. Ash didn't think she'd given her mother their new address after that second move last year, but wasn't there a fire department just up the road somewhere?

Ash had screamed for help quite a bit. The apartment complex was fairly secluded, wedged in by hills and busy backroads and a small tributary that nobody traveled because it hit a dead end a little past the apartment. Her neighbors had been unusually quiet—even Melanie had seemed to finally be content with the arrangement of her picture frames and put the hammer to rest—but, then again, maybe it wasn't so unusual. Maybe they were all dead. But that hadn't stopped her from screaming herself hoarse—swearing at the men who had done this to her, at fucking Doug; then screaming for help from someone, anyone, from *God* . . . and then a voice had answered her.

Not God.

Mo.

"You girls all right in there?"

Ash had rushed to the far wall of pocked stone and called out his name.

"Yes, it's just me. How are you, Ashley?"

She'd had to stifle a laugh at the question, afraid it would morph into a sob. How was she? Only Mo, their stolid kindly grandpa of a neighbor, would ask something so mundane during such a clearly fucked situation. A pandemic, a state in lock-down, and now a landlord who had effectively imprisoned them and left them to die, and here Mo was asking how *Ash* was doing today and isn't the weather nice.

"Did I lose you, Ashley, dear?"

"No, I'm here," she called back. She had to raise her voice substantially to be heard through the solid rock, and it hurt after all her screaming. Mo would have had to as well, being normally so soft-spoken. She imagined this might be the loudest Mo had raised his voice in years. "I'm not doing very well, Mo," she said. "Yourself?" She smiled at herself, at the absurdity—she'd taken on his neighborly small-talk tone, just moments after screaming herself hoarse about dying here and how all landlords should rot in Hell.

"I'm just fine, thank you, all things considered," Mo replied.

"Were you . . . ?" She couldn't finish the words. How would she even describe it? *Were you woken in the middle of the night by the sounds of the last nails hammered into your coffin?*

"Locked inside?" Mo finished mercifully. "Yes, it seems you and I share in that particular pickle."

Ash giggled helplessly. She sat on the carpet and

leaned against the wall. It was the closest she'd felt to another human since . . . well, since she and Jack had made love. This was calmer, more peaceful. Mo had that effect. Even on the other side of a wall, she still felt protected by those kind eyes.

"I'd imagine," Mo said, "there's no use asking you about your prospects?"

"No prospects, Mo. We're stuck."

"Never mind that. Tell me, how's Jacqueline?"

Ash wiped an errant tear away. "She's . . ."

What could she say? What *should* she say?

In their admittedly brief conversations, Mo had shown a surprising interest in their well-being, and had never been afraid to broach topics most semi-strangers would have seen as taboo. He'd once said to Ash, seemingly out of the blue, *You know, sometimes the best we can do for our loved ones is to kiss them and tell them it's okay to do what they want to do.* Somehow he'd known of their inner marital struggle, known that Ash had been trying to get Jack to come to a party her company was hosting, that Jack had rebuffed every single attempt. Armed with his words of wisdom, Ash had walked into the apartment, told Jack she wasn't going to the party, and huddled with her to watch Jack's favorite ghost-hunting reality show all night. It had been a brief lovely lull in the Texas storm of their married life.

So now she found herself being more honest with Mo than perhaps she'd been with herself. "Jack's not okay, Mo. She needs help that I can't give her."

There was a pause as Mo considered this. "Oh?"

And they talked. Ash didn't know how long—minutes, hours? And she didn't know how much, if any,

Jack had heard, despite Ash's raised voice. She frankly doubted Jack's ability to follow any conversations right now, even the ones about her. It was the first time in a long time that Ash had said anything and everything she hadn't even known she was bottling up. About her worries and anxieties, about her utter failure at starting a new life for her and Jack here in Texas, but mostly about how afraid she was for her wife. And maybe *of* her wife.

After a while, she heard Mo's voice change directions and realized he was standing. "It sounds to me, dear girl, like you've been carrying much more on your shoulders than you should. Ashley deserves Ashley." Before she could ask him what that last cryptic comment meant, he added, "And all you needed to do was ask for help. I accept."

She stood as well. "Accept what? What do you mean?"

"There's no escaping your apartment without your love, Ashley," Mo replied. "On that we agree. My love has left me, years ago now, and I am happy with the decisions I have made. They shall allow me now to escape here unburdened and bring back help."

Ash was speechless. Her brain was stuck on something he said about his "love"—his love left him? Did he mean divorce? She knew so little about her quiet neighbor, and she'd just assumed that if he'd ever married then his partner had passed away and he was waiting to meet them in another life. How presumptuous of her.

"My dear, are you still there?"

"Yes," she said, "but—"

"Listen carefully, then. With just the barest amount of pressure with a sharp point at its center, this glass sliding door will shatter in its frame. Cheap glass just needs an excuse to fall apart. I will then abseil down to ground level. I do not expect any of our cars in the parking lot to have been left drivable, but I'm hoping my canoe is where I left it. If so, I will be taking my canoe down the river. "

"But—"

"Please, listen close. I'm afraid I'll lose my nerve if you let me. Once I've reached sufficient distance for my cellular to once again have reception, I will be able to make calls and set up an emergency retrieval for you and Jacqueline and perhaps any others who find themselves trapped in this infernal place."

There was a beat of silence.

"Do I still have you with me, my girl?"

Ash swallowed and found her voice. "Y-yes."

She couldn't distinguish his reply through the thick stone. He seemed to be muttering to himself as he moved away from the wall. Ash listened, her heart in her throat, and when nothing happened she thought he'd left her.

"Mo?"

His voice, at a distance: "We'll be okay, Ashley."

Then, the sound of shattering glass. Ash jumped at the noise. It was all happening so quickly. Was Mo really breaking out through his own sliding-door window? She couldn't imagine the kind old man doing something so . . . heroic. But now she heard several muted thumps, and she thought this might be Mo climbing out of the hole in his wall and rappelling down. Crunching glass, cinching rope, heavy stomps, and it was all happening so *fast*.

We'll be okay, Ashley.

That's what he'd said, and now she was certain he was

right. In a moment that seemed to stretch forever, she felt a frisson of hope like electricity jolting her heart back to life after so long dead. She saw the future spooled out before her: a SWAT team taking a battering ram to the door, breaking it down easily, like a cane field in a high wind; her and Jack rescued, watching as fucking hand-cuffed Doug was frog-marched into the back of the sheriff's SUV; an ambulance wailing off into the night, Ash's wife safely inside, just a few miles from full medical care . . .

All thanks to Mo.

She could still hear him rappelling down. She rushed to see him through her own sliding-door window, to see those crunching boots and cinching rope and crinkly smile—

Then the gunfire drowned everything out.

Ash dropped to the carpet, still halfway to the window, waiting for silence.

The guns kept firing.

She screamed—or thought she screamed; she couldn't tell.

Still the guns blazed.

It was like they had been waiting for him. For all she knew, they probably were. All those men, fucking Doug's men, down on the ground, stockpiled with all the guns the great state of Texas could provide. All those guns exploding into action at the same time. A thundering, concussive *BOOM!* louder than any thunderclap, louder than anything she'd ever experienced, shaking the very floor beneath her. She felt the carpet quake, everywhere a wall of sound, a sound swallowing Mo like the maw of a sea monster. The sound was everything, it was more than a sound, it was the world, blotting Ashley out; her moment of hope, seeming to last forever only moments ago, was a speck of moondust in that sound.

The guns roared without breath.

She sobbed, screamed, but she couldn't hear her own cries.

Mo was dead.

There was no one.

NOW, ALONE, ASHLEY STARED at her reflection, the job done. Her hair, her old self, lay shed all around her.

No birthday song for her.

Only the memory of gunfire.

12

JACQUELINE

"Police Brutality Reaches Fever Pitch, Protests and Riots Erupt Across America Despite On-going Pandemic"

—headlines everywhere
June 2020

"White House Supports Our Nation's Great Police Force, Gives Support for Aggressive Military Action Against ANTIFA"

—FOX News
June 2020

JACK WAS NOT ALONE.

Someone else was in the dark bedroom. It wasn't Ashley. She knew everything about Ash's body in bed: the weight and the smell and all her little mannerisms. This was someone else, someone larger.

And they were climbing toward her.

She pushed herself up, her bandaged feet carefully propped at the end of the bed.

"Who's there?"

Her voice was cracked from disuse. She cleared it.

"Ash . . . ?"

The figure didn't respond, just slithered under the comforter, filling the spot Ash used to occupy back when they still slept in the same bed.

"Who are you?" she whispered into the black.

Still no reply, and it was impossible in the bedroom's darkness to distinguish anything other than an amorphous shape filling the shadows under the comforter. Something small crawled out from the shape, toward her.

She froze in fear.

What is it? her mind gibbered. *What does it want?*

The thing that peeked out from under the comforter didn't have any blinking or staring eyes she could see. Sinuous legs extended from its body, and they wriggled as it crawled. It was roughly the shape of—

It was a hand. The hand of whoever had climbed into bed with her. Its fingers danced their way over the sheets and paused at her thigh before tickling onto her skin.

No . . .

But a part of her watched raptly. A part of her didn't *want* to stop the hand, to stop whoever it was attached to it. A part of her wanted to know how that hand felt on her skin.

The fingers felt rough, callused; she sensed strength behind them. The hand applied more pressure as it climbed her thigh. Butterflies—or moths or cicadas—swirled in her tummy.

Still she didn't move, didn't stop the hand.

She held her breath.

Her heart was a hammer in her throat.

The hand still moved like an enormous spider. A thick

blue vein, barely visible in the dark, pulsed on what would be the spider's abdomen. Its legs scratched up her thigh, ever closer to her panties, where it paused. It was close enough now that she could see the coarse hairs bristling between the joints of the squirming legs. After a beat of rest, as if waiting to see if she would stop it, the spider progressed.

Tickling her panty line.

Jack's breath hitched.

Then onto the cotton fabric and back to the skin on the other side.

The butterflies burst in a new swarm as the spider's legs brushed across that patch of skin between her panties and her belly button. Ash used to love tickling that spot. It was her "I want to have sex, how 'bout you?" move, to lightly graze her fingers over that swath of sensitive skin.

The spider was now pulling itself up her stomach. Past her belly button and over her abdomen. There was something sensual in the way its hairy legs twitched and dug themselves into her pale skin; they pressed a barely audible moan from her, rushing past her lips on heated, escaping air.

The spider reached her breasts. It stopped, then raised one quivering leg hesitantly toward her left breast, as if asking permission.

"Yes," she breathed.

The spider's raised leg, almost vibrating in anticipation, inched over to her nipple and circled, its coarse hairs tickling her nipple erect. She moaned again. Growing bolder, it climbed atop her bare breast. It lay itself flat, pressing its bloated abdomen against her breast. She moaned louder, longer.

Something about this struck her as funny. What was it? *The legs,* a voice in her head whispered. *Count the legs.*

Count the legs?

The spider pressed itself against her, harder, harder. Its legs now circled her entire breast, and they constricted. Her moan rose again.

The voice in her head said, *Spiders have eight legs.*

Huh? Eight . . . ?

The spider squeezed her breast harder.

Her pleasure morphed into pain.

No spider. A hand. A large, hairy, rough hand.

As if conjured by this thought, the hand's wrist and forearm and elbow and bicep materialized in the dark. Connected to the arm and the hand clutching at her was the thing, the someone, and they rose from the bedding. Eyes shone out from under the comforter. A grin of gleaming teeth, impossibly large, a Cheshire smile of ivory tombstones.

Still frozen, her moan climbed, edging on a scream.

Another spider shot out from the comforter. The grinning someone closed it tight over her mouth and nose so that she couldn't breathe, his other hand still gripping her breast.

"Give us a kiss, Jackie boy," the Cardigan Man said. "I need it."

No! her mind blared, *no! no! no!*

She snaked one hand out, clutched at a corner of the comforter, and yanked it up and away, whipping it off the someone underneath—the Cardigan Man, she knew now, but how could he have gotten in here?

The space beneath the comforter, now exposed, was empty.

Her nose and mouth were suddenly free. Her breath hissed past her teeth in sharp gasps.

She was alone.

"No," she said to the empty room, her voice still hoarse. "No, he was just here, he was *here*."

She scrambled up, throwing the bedspread clear of the mattress, and scrambled across the bed. Her palms hissed across the sheets as if she'd feel him underneath, sewn into the mattress like that one Quentin Tarantino movie Ash had shown her. Not finding him there, she stumbled from the bed, falling awkwardly, and crawled on her knees so her bandaged heels wouldn't touch the floor.

"Where are you? *Where are you?*"

She threw the detritus strewn across the bedroom floor, frantically searching for him. For anyone. For the spider. She didn't know. Was she losing her mind? No, she saw him, she *felt* him. Her boob still hurt from his grip; she still felt the imprint of his palm against her mouth.

She continued to search the room in the dark, bursting about on her hands and knees like an injured crab. As she disturbed the many little hillocks of abandoned towels and clothes and remnants of meals from who knew when, she became vaguely aware of a briny, eye-watering stench woken up from beneath the dirty laundry.

She stopped.

Nobody had moved through this room in days. Weeks, maybe. What day *was* it? What *month*? Fuck if she knew. The point being, the Cardigan Man didn't come into this room. It had just been a vivid dream. A nightmare.

She was alone.

Or was she? How could she *know*? She couldn't. All she could trust were her own senses. She'd known what she'd seen at the end of the breezeway, and Ash had been *wrong*, it *was* the Cardigan Man. And just now, in bed, that hadn't *felt* like a dream—hadn't felt like a nightmare, either, because hadn't she *liked* his hand on her chest? Hadn't she *liked* his fingers coming dangerously close to her crotch, liked them teasing and circling her nipple?

She had. And on top of that, she'd known the whole time that it wasn't Ash. She'd known that someone other than her wife had crawled into bed with her . . . and she *liked* it.

Did that make her a horrible person?

She collapsed on the bedroom floor, feeling the musty carpet and nebulous laundry cushioning her. She had known it wasn't Ash, and what's more, she'd known it was a man. A big, gruff man with callused hands and taut, muscular arms . . . and maybe a small part of her even knew *which* man that hand belonged to.

What had he said to her, all those months ago, down by the river?

"Then maybe I'll show you a good time."

Is that what he was here to do now? He and Doug had had their fun shutting the biracial lesbos inside, and now he'd come in to . . . fuck her straight?

If that were true . . . what did he do to Ash first?

"No," she said to herself, groaning on the floor.

Remember the mess, she told herself. *Nobody has walked in here. Nobody has opened that door.*

She was close enough to it to see there was a heap pressed up against the bottom of the door, undisturbed. It opened inward. No one had opened that door recently.

Which meant no one had crawled into her bed and felt her up.

Which meant the Cardigan Man had not come back to show her a good time.

And did that fact really make her feel . . . disappointment?

Before she could explore this feeling more, something occurred to her, spiking her already-racing heart with another shot of adrenaline. Her boob still tingled, her mouth the same; the butterflies came back to life.

"The closet!" she exclaimed.

She burst back into action. Of course—he hadn't come in through the main door. He'd wanted to surprise her, to sneak up on her, so of course he would come in through the connecting bathroom door.

But she knew this was ridiculous even before she got to the bathroom. She froze, on her knees in the walk-in closet, breathing heavily, drenched in sweat.

There was no Cardigan Man waiting for her in the bathroom, drawing her a bath.

She was still trapped in this hellhole, starving to death.

"I'll give you something to eat, bitch," a voice said behind her.

She froze. It had come from the bedroom.

"Turn around and I'll feed it to you," the voice growled.

She couldn't move. She was suddenly hyperaware of her bandaged heels, spread out behind her, vulnerable to the Cardigan Man's stomping boots.

"Or don't," he continued. "I should have known you'd prefer it from behind."

She whimpered.

The voice teased: "I'm coming . . ."

Her paralysis broke and she rolled to her side, disappearing behind the racks of hanging clothes. She scrambled up, hidden in the folds of clothing, feeling her bandaged heels press into the carpet but not caring, too jacked up on fight-or-flight to be aware of any pain from her wounds. She couldn't hear him coming toward her, but she knew she needed a weapon before it was too late. Scenarios from every home-invasion movie Ash had ever shown her flashed through her mind like a sizzle reel. The best she could find from her surroundings was a stiletto heel—Ash's, never worn but bought in the hopes of glamorous company shindigs in Austin high rises and ballrooms.

She brandished the stiletto in both hands, the heel pointing out, and willed her heart to slow down, tried to steady her breath so she could hear. She could picture him out there, filling the bedroom's doorframe with his neatly trimmed beard and *Helter Skelter* T-shirt: standing perfectly still, to trick her, to make her think she was alone, to gaslight her into thinking she was just overreacting to the dying echoes of a lucid dream . . . waiting for her to crawl back out with her guard down, waiting for the moment that he could fall on her and return one powerful hand to her mouth and the other to her breast and take her right then and there, on the closet's carpeted floor.

Time passed. Minutes . . . hours. The timelessness of life in a pandemic returned, leaving her feeling as if she'd been hiding in this closet with a stiletto clutched in her hands for ages, all day and all night and into the next morning.

Finally, when the pain from her heels broke the barrier of her dissolving energy spike, she had to move. She edged out from the wall of clothes and peeked toward the bedroom.

Nothing.

Nobody.

She was alone.

Entirely alone.

Again she collapsed on the closet floor, chucking the stiletto into a shadowy corner.

No Cardigan Man.

No Ashley.

No Jack.

13

ASHLEY

Whoever thought to call this thing a "novel coronavirus" is a criminal mastermind. No way was our illiterate President ever going to read something that sounds like a book. #Trump-CantRead #HeHasTheBestWords

@BooksCanSaveTheWorld

9:59 PM · June 12, 2020

431 RTs 2.5K likes

Dear Diary,

Ash stopped and stared at what she'd written. *Dear Diary*—for fuck's sake, she sounded like a teenage girl on prom night. She reminded herself that was just because she hadn't written in this journal in a while, and continued:

A lot's happened since last we spoke. Even saying it sounds laughable. "A lot's happened," what a fucking joke. A <u>LOT</u> has happened, like, the-world-is-ending levels of "a lot." Not even exaggerating.

She sat with her back against the sliding-door window.

After what happened to Mo, she'd been petrified of showing her face to anyone who may be out there watching. Even just thinking of that sliding-glass door sent bursts of gunfire through her memory until she'd clamped both hands to her ears and screwed her eyes shut.

But then the power went out. She wasn't sure when—the days and nights had all since melded together like some kind of big ball of wibbly-wobbly, timey-wimey stuff. She figured fucking Doug had realized he didn't have to keep paying for electricity if he'd already consigned his remaining tenants to their deaths. Luckily for her, he'd somehow forgotten—or maybe he just didn't care either way, or, better yet, maybe he was dead—to turn off other utilities. The gas stove still worked; the water still ran, though without heat.

Most of their days were dark now. Well, she supposed *all* of Jack's days were dark, holed up in that bedroom with the shades drawn and blankets piled atop her. But even out here it was dark. The big sliding-glass door was their only window in the main living area; it looked out on a ravine shadowed by the building on one side and a climbing scree of hill on the other. What little sunlight reached them only shone directly in for a couple hours in the morning, and even then it was filtered through countless branches and leaves from the towering Texas ash trees.

After she'd overcome her fear of meeting Mo's same fate, Ashley had crawled to the glass window, desperate to feel any amounts of direct sunlight on her face. She wasn't like Jack—she couldn't stay inside for days on end without feeling like she might crawl out of her skin from pent-up energy. She needed fresh air, or, if that wasn't possible—just a single pane of glass away and yet entire planets out of reach—she at least needed sunlight.

In those seconds after showing her face in the window, she flinched, expecting bullets to tear into her, expecting to die in the same thundering maelstrom that had swallowed Mo . . . but nothing happened. She choked on a nervous giggle, chastised herself for being just as needlessly afraid as Jack. Of course they wouldn't shoot at her. She was obeying their rules—she was staying inside. No Boy Scout trip for her, no rappelling escape like Mo's. Heroics had gotten Mo killed. But not Ash. Not Ashley. She was a good little tenant: She paid her rent on time. She didn't smoke on the walkway. She didn't cause any noise complaints. And she stayed inside when a team of mysterious killers locked up the whole building as tight as a crypt and guarded it with an army's arsenal.

Relieved at being awarded this one pleasure, direct sunlight, she spent much of her days pressed up against the glass or sitting nearby. Now, she had her back to the glass, notebook on her knees, so that she could use the precious sunshine to write by.

How do I even begin? Trust me, Diary, it'll sound like the voice-over for a big Hollywood blockbuster disaster movie, but it's all true.

It started with a deadly virus. First in China, so you can guess how many dumbass Texans have decided yours truly is directly responsible. It quickly spread everywhere else, and since America is run by greedy idiots who defunded every program set up for this exact kind of emergency, we were basically fucked from the start.

Oh wow, I just realized you don't even know we're in Texas now. It's been a while, Diary. But you know how Jack is. Or was . . .

No, she's not dead, though sometimes I wonder. Sometimes I wake up on the couch and wonder if today's the day I'm going to peek into the bedroom and see a cloud of flies dancing over a corpse that used to be my wife.

Jesus H. Christ, I must sound heartless.

We have a lot to catch up on, Diary.

Finding the journal in the darkness had been surprisingly easy. After living without electricity for long enough, you forget how you used to rely on certain senses. She hadn't even considered waiting for daylight, had just struck out in the middle of the night when the whim had first hit. Gone to the hallway closet and felt her way up to a specific box high up in the corner. She was strong, maybe stronger now than she'd ever been, what with all the balls of timey-wimey boredom during which she'd drop down and do a set of push-ups or crunchies or she'd do lunges from one end of the room to the other until she could feel her heart vibrating through her body like a tuning fork. Not to mention the forced diet of rationed, dwindling food supplies. It wasn't a healthy balanced meal, but it sure did strip away the fat. So pulling that heavy box down from the closet's shelf in absolute darkness had been an easy thing.

When had she finally given in to Jack's jealousy and boxed all her journals away? She couldn't remember. Sometime before Texas, sometime in California, and for some reason she'd lugged the box all the way to Austin.

Maybe a small part of her expected—or at least hoped—
to unpack this integral piece of herself someday.

> *I keep thinking about my mom, Diary. The last
> time we talked was . . . not great. She was pushing me
> to come home, and I just got sick of it. I said some cruel
> things . . . but I didn't mean it. Everyone says things
> they don't mean if they know they'll have a chance to
> apologize later, right?*
>
> *She wanted me to come home <u>without</u> Jack. Dad's
> orders, probably. That's what caused the fight. Telling
> your daughter she can come home, but your <u>other</u> daugh-
> ter has to stay away, smack dab in the apocalypse?
> What the fuck, Mom? Sure, they're a little old-fash-
> ioned, but our family is still a <u>family</u>. We stick with
> each other. No matter what.*
>
> *Great. Now I'm crying.*
>
> *I didn't used to cry this much.*
>
> *Writing to you always used to help me think
> through things, Diary. I miss that. Sometimes you just
> can't see something fully, from every angle and perspec-
> tive, until you've written it out in ink and clarified your
> thoughts until your hand starts to cramp. I wish I hadn't
> put you away for so long.*
>
> *I think I've been thinking about my parents a lot,
> about that final phone call with my mom, so that I don't
> think about Mo. Poor Mo . . .*
>
> *Mo was my neighbor, Diary. He was so kind. I
> didn't realize it until he was gone, but he'd become some-
> what of a father figure for me, in his own quiet way. I
> mean, I love my dad, but Mo held this sense of . . .
> <u>acceptance</u> . . . something I've always wanted but never*

quite received from Dad. The few times I'd had a con-
versation with Mo, I never felt like my sexuality was
some taboo thing, a part of me he'd rather ignore and
pretend didn't exist. It was simply a part of who I am
that Mo never seemed uncomfortable acknowledging
when he'd ask me how my wife was doing or when he'd
suggest new recipes I could try for a "date night." I had
a dream last night that it was my wedding again, but
this time I had a father's offered arm to hold as I walked
down the aisle. I mean, my dad was at my real wedding,
sure, but he hadn't done that. Mom told me not to even
ask. But in my dream, I looked up and it was Mo,
smiling down at me. His kind eyes crinkling the way
they did.

And a third eye, perfectly between them. An eye of
welling blood.

A bullet hole.

Oh, Mo . . . I'm so sorry.

He died trying to help me, Diary. Trying to help
me because I wouldn't leave Jack.

Just like my mom—hurt by the words of her daugh-
ter because I wouldn't leave Jack.

Ash stopped. Dropped the pen from numb fingers.
Threw the journal across the room.

She was afraid of writing more. Afraid of where it
might lead.

She'd always told herself she put away that journal—
put away *all* the journals, the stacks she'd filled every day
since she was a little girl—because of what it was doing
to Jack. When they'd first moved in together, Jack had
asked her so many questions about what she was writing

every day . . . until Ash had finally snapped back at her and they'd fought about it. Jack was certain that Ash was sitting there every day, detailing all of Jack's faults. "What could you possibly have to write about every day?" she'd asked, but what she'd really meant was *What could you possibly have to write about every day besides me, me, all about me, and if you can't tell me then it must be bad, you must be writing about how you hate me and you find me ugly and repulsive and you think I'm stupid and me, me, me?*

After months of fights about it, there'd been a time when she wrote in the journal less frequently, as a compromise. But she'd found that she suddenly had less to say. So she'd put it all away, in a box that she'd shoved into all the closets of their lives.

But what if she was lying to herself? It wasn't Jack's paranoia that made her fall out of the habit . . . but rather, it was her own thoughts. Avoiding the journal meant avoiding certain epiphanies she was afraid of collecting from the depths of her subconscious, her internal self.

Epiphanies like the one that was making her hands shake right now.

No . . . no, Ashley. Don't think about that.

She curled her spine against the glass window, lowering her head to her knees. She pressed her hands against her scalp, trying to stop them from shaking, and rasped her fingers over the sparse growth on her shaved head.

"Don't think about it," she told herself. "Just put it in a cardboard box and shove it in the closet."

She didn't even know what she was talking about anymore. The journal, or the very thoughts in her brain.

Her head still in her hands, she dropped her knees down into a butterfly position, thinking she'd do yoga or something—maybe that would calm her, just more exercise like a too-small band-aid over a festering wound—and her left knee bumped into something blocking its way.

She lifted her head to look. It was the cardboard box full of her old stuff.

She turned, pressing her ear and cheek to the cool glass of the window, and flipped the box open. Rifled through its contents: stacks of old journals, filled with black ink and blue ink and pink ink (in a pink journal, from when she was nine and pink was her favorite color and thus needed to be everywhere); her old biology textbook; and her old paperbacks, beat up with use and love. She pulled the books out one at a time, smiling at each.

Fahrenheit 451.

Nineteen Eighty-Four.

Sea Monsters.

The Stand. She laughed. A huge Stephen King novel about a scary pandemic unleashed upon an unprepared America. The paperback was practically falling apart. Should she read it again, see if Grandpa Steve had any apocalypse pointers for her?

Her smile grew as she emptied the box. All these journals filled with her thoughts, filled with her anxieties and fears and excitements and hopes for the future . . . filled with who she used to be.

Where had that Ashley gone?

That was a person so distant from her life now that it was almost impossible to picture: still vivacious, yes, always full of energy, but also somehow able to sit still long enough to devour all of these books—*horror* books, most of them, something she'd almost forgotten—and oh so independent. Jack had been the first person she'd ever settled down with; before her, Ash had dated around, yes, but she'd never let herself fall into any kind of routine that depended on someone else. She'd been driven, determined to make something of herself, and as far as she was concerned, if she ever got married then that person had better be someone who would support her but understand how to not get in the way, someone who would enjoy the ride and let Ashley drive.

But hadn't that been her relationship with Jack to an extent? Yes . . . and no. Yes, they'd moved to Austin because of Ashley's career, but it hadn't been a *career* so much as it had been a *good-paying job*, and Jack had been desperate to get out of her hometown anyway. Jack didn't care where they went—and maybe that had somehow helped Ash fall into the role of always taking care of Jack . . . she was the one who made the decisions not because they were the decisions she wanted to make, but because if she didn't then nobody would. Even then, if she didn't make the so-called *right* decisions, she could feel Jack's disappointment like accidentally walking into a spiderweb—you couldn't see it, but you could feel it stretching across the skin and getting into your mouth.

No. Don't think about that. Box it away.

At the very bottom of the cardboard box she found a photo. She stared at it, smiling. And then her smile burned, and the tears began to fall afresh. One broke away from her cheek and raced down the glass pane of the window.

Great—more crying.

The photo was of her high school graduation. There she was, barely an adult, in her cap and gown, the tip of the tassel died hot pink to match the tips of her hair. She remembered this moment. Her dad was behind the camera, and the photo captured his daughter and his wife hugging each other, laughing.

No Jack. And she'd buried the photo away. Along with all the journals of her old self.

"I'm sorry," she told her younger self, told her mom. Told Jack.

I'm sorry.

14

JACQUELINE & ASHLEY

Headline: VP Pence Ignores Hospital Mask Regulations During Visit, Is Rumored to Have Contracted COVID-19

—reddit.com
/r/WellWellWellIfItIsntTheConsequences
OfMyOwnActions

"Jailed Protestors Are Living In a COVID Hotbed and Being Starved to the Point of Hallucination and Agonizing Death"

—headline from *The Hill*
June 2020

MORGAN KINER WAS SHOWING JACK pictures of mangled bodies.

They'd never had a computer in the bedroom before—Ash had suggested they keep any screens from the bedroom to help with their sleep and "together time" (this was years ago, when they actually made an effort to *have* together time)—but here it was now, on a big desk shoved in the corner where the dresser used to be. Maybe Ash got rid of the dresser when Jack was sleeping; after all, a dresser was just wasted space if you kept all your clothes scattered across the carpet, right? She wasn't sure where Ash had found this big-ass desk, what with them being quarantined inside their apartment like the rest of the city—the state, the country, the world, who knew?—but it scratched a certain familiar itch in her limbic system . . . she could feel it crawling around in there, scuttling across her temporal lobes like a cockroach, until it burrowed its nest directly into the warm center of her brain, the hippocampus.

A memory . . . what was it?

"Dude," Morgan said, the computer screen painting her face a ghostly blue, "come look at this gnarly shit."

A spike of alarm shot through Jack. She felt the knee-jerk urge to hiss, *Don't swear, Mom'll hear you!*

She paused. *Mom . . . ?*

And then she knew. That itch in her brain was because she *knew* this desk, the big, boxy kind with the rolling partition that could be closed and locked tight like a Spencer's Gifts at the strip mall. But not just this *kind* of desk; this *exact one.* Her mom must have given them the desk—maybe as a wedding present, such a backhanded hand-me-down gift, as if to say, *Well, it was destined for the garbage heap anyway.* Yes, that must be it; Jack had just forgotten. Ash must have included the desk with the few pieces of furniture they'd had moved from California to Austin and she'd set it up while Jack slept; she'd set it up as a surprise, as a gift, maybe a sort of peace offering after all their time ignoring each other.

She remembered every inch of this desk well, but not fondly. It had sat in the kitchen of her childhood home, of all places. This was intentional on her mother's part, Jack knew, so that she could catch her child if she were ever dumb enough—*sinful* enough—to use the family computer to look up the four-syllable sin . . . *porn-o-graph-y*. Her mother had often feigned kitchen chores so that she could keep watch over that desk, her shining eyes just waiting to pin Jack down and say, *I know what you think about when no one's looking . . . JESUS knows what you think about . . . JESUS knows you undress women in your head, you OGLE them and desire to CARESS them with your dirty little LESBO fingers . . .*

She'd never actually *said* any of those things to her daughter. But her eyes did, every time she looked at Jack while in the kitchen. Besides, she didn't need to say them—her husband and brother-in-law said everything to little Jacqueline plenty for all of them.

"Psst!" It was Morgan again. "Hey, butt fuck, come *here*."

Jack moaned as she again swallowed those words—*Mom'll hear you!*—and slid across the mattress so she could get closer to the desk and look over Morgan's shoulder.

But it wasn't Ash's laptop Morgan was browsing on. It was the bulky desktop monitor—again from her childhood, just like this desk—and she knew that if she were to lean down she'd see tucked beneath the desk the dusty computer tower, with its disc drive and blipping green read-outs like little eyes. Tiny, blinking, radioactive-green eyes her mother had installed especially for her little Jacqueline, to spy on her sins.

Had her mother gifted them this Stone Age computer

too?

To spy on little Jacqueline and her *lesbo* wife?

No, that didn't make sense . . .

And then her eyes focused on the screen.

She wanted to scream.

"Isn't this *cool?*" Morgan gushed, her voice a triumphant crow. "Can you imagine something like this happening to you?"

It was a Google Images page full of mangled bodies. Specifically, bodies that had been mangled by the teeth of a shark. Morgan had typed, in the search bar at the top of the page, *Shark Attack Wounds*. And now she was scrolling through hundreds of close-up, high-definition photographs of body parts missing pieces of themselves, bodies stapled and stitched back to some semblance of the human form.

"I turned off the Safety search," Morgan said, happily scrolling away.

Blood. Red everywhere, and in some places a yellow pus, or blood that had turned black, or skin that had turned gangrenous, different mottled colors like countries on a map. Stitches tracing bite marks like the dotted lines of an anatomy chart.

This wasn't the first time Morgan Kiner had shown her these images. She'd done it years ago when they were kids, on this very computer and desk, in Jack's childhood kitchen. Jack remembered spending the entire ten or fifteen minutes in a tug-of-war between two emotions: fear that her mother would come marching into the kitchen and see them staring at images of naked body parts or hear Morgan saying the F word or the S-H word or the B word . . . and fascinated horror at what she saw on the computer screen, at the little girl who seemed to be missing not just her arm but her entire shoulder, at the man her dad's age whose nose was missing and in its place were a few staples that just kind of held together a lumpy patch of skin in the middle of his face.

But she couldn't tell Morgan to stop, not back then when they were just kids, eleven or twelve or so, and not now, in Austin, in the dark of her bedroom. She liked Morgan. What's more, back when they were kids she was pretty sure she *like*-liked Morgan, though she never admitted it to herself. She hadn't openly admitted those kinds of emotions outside of the murky swamp water of her subconscious and her night thoughts until a year or so after Morgan, to a girl named Sarah Jenkins. But Morgan Kiner had had this magnetism about her. Jack liked how she made her feel—always on the edge of committing some great sin that would finally set her free from her mother's claws, from Jesus's claws, even. Morgan was unpredictable, which was exciting, but mainly she bossed Jack around in a way that felt different from the bossing around at the hands of her mom. Morgan made exciting, daring decisions so that Jack didn't have to, and then she pushed Jack into action.

Like these photos. Where else would she get the chance to see such gnarly shit as this?

Turned out she'd get that chance almost a decade later, when her new girlfriend found out she'd never seen her absolute favorite movie. *Jaws*. It was a classic, Ash said, and Jack just *had* to watch it.

And when they reached the part where the shark first visited the crowded beach—thanks to the greedy blowhard mayor, played by Murray Hamilton, who resembled a certain idiot-in-chief from today—and gobbled that little boy down off his floatie . . . Jack had clutched Ashley in terror, her mind flashing to those grotesque images Morgan Kiner had shown her all those years ago.

Looking at the images again, now, over Morgan's shoulder in the dark bedroom, Jack felt another itch, this one not in her brain but somewhere on her body. The more she looked at the pictures of the shark bites, the shredded skin like pasta and marinera, the more she itched . . . somewhere low, below the waist. She reached one hand absentmindedly down her side, past her knee, until her fingers grazed—

She screamed. She looked down. Suddenly, in the dark, she could see as clear as day: a shark had taken a big bite out of her heel. It was bandaged, but sopping wet with some kind of discharge, sloughing off her foot like the seasoned skin off a piece of pan-fried chicken.

"Pretty gnarly shit, huh?" Morgan Kiner said.

She looked up. Was Morgan talking about her foot? Was *this* "gnarly shit"?

But it wasn't Morgan Kiner at the computer desk anymore.

It was the Cardigan Man, his voice muffled behind his gasmask.

It was the Cardigan Man—and then it wasn't—and then it was again. The person sitting before her flickered like channels on a busted television. Morgan Kiner, then the Cardigan Man, then his face boiling away and then bitten as if from a shark, and then—

And then her wife. Ash. Wearing the Cardigan Man's gasmask and leering at her.

"What kind of shark you think that could be?"

Morgan then Ashley then Morgan asked, then, the flickering coming to a staticky stop, the Cardigan Man, his eyes gleaming down at her foot. "Hammerhead? Great white? Megalodon?" He laughed, a coughing grind she felt in her own lungs like breathed-in asbestos. "You oughta get that looked at, Jackie boy."

He killed the computer screen, plunging them into darkness.

ASH WAS MAKING A PEACE OFFERING: pan-fried chicken.

It was a bit of a miracle that they even had chicken to fry. *A quarantine miracle,* she called it. When the power had first been shut off—what, maybe three weeks ago? Who the fuck knew. Miracles, as a rule, didn't let little technicalities like linear time get in the way. When the power had first been shut off, one of the things Ash had been sure to do was take care of the fridge. Thankfully, she'd already filled the freezer with tons of ice cubes, thinking maybe Jack would need them for her feet, so she'd just removed the ice cream and shut the rest tightly inside and had herself a little cry over spoonfuls of rocky road. Somehow, in all the craziness, she'd forgotten about the food inside the freezer after that. When she tentatively peeked inside earlier today she'd expected the sharp smell of melted, spoiled waste, of something *dead.* And sure, there was some of that, but shoved in the very back were a few chicken thighs that were still cold and, as far as she could tell, still edible.

Writing in her journal had been rejuvenating. After her little stroll down memory lane with her cardboard box full of books and that graduation photo, she'd retrieved her journal back from where she'd flung it and resumed writing. She wrote so much that her hand cramped. She hadn't done this in so long, and something kicked on inside her, like a generator, and the floodgates *whooshed* open.

With it came an epiphany. She wasn't going to be her mom. She wasn't going to let unspoken words stagnate in her marriage. She wasn't going to let Jack keep her frozen in place, even when they were stuck inside an apartment-turned-prison. Even if they were most likely going to die here. If that was the case, then so be it: but they'd do that together, as Ashley and Jacqueline, married through sickness and health. Till death would they part, right?

She hummed while she cooked the spitting chicken thighs over the gas stove. After all the crying and the writing and the sunlight by the window, she felt husked out. Renewed and ready to finally have the hard conversations, even if Jack wasn't.

Peace offering in hand, Ashley went to the bedroom—not through the bedroom door, which she knew was stopped up by mounds of dirty laundry on the other side, but through the bathroom. She knocked on the little pocket door leading to the walk-in closet. Sometimes Jack liked to huddle up inside the closet; Ash didn't want to start this peace offering off on the wrong foot by barging in on Jack's "sanctuary" unannounced.

Jack's voice, muffled: "What do you want."

Not a question, and not friendly. She was glad she knocked.

"I bring food, baby. Your favorite. I thought you could use some good protein."

Jack said something indistinguishable through the

closed door.

Ash slid the door open a few inches on its track. "Pan-fried chicken, babe."

No response from Jack.

Ash opened the door just far enough to fit the plate, with its two chicken thighs and napkin and fork and knife—she'd hesitated with that last piece, wondering if it would be safe to give Jack a knife in her current state of mind, then dismissed the thought, scolding herself for treating her wife like a child again—and she set it on the carpeted floor. As she did, a smell hit her full in the face. She bit down a gag, almost vomiting onto the plate of miracle food. It reminded her of the smell she'd prepared herself to find in the thawed-out freezer: acrid yet tangy, like old kombucha stirred to a paste with goose shit. What *was* that? If she hadn't heard Jack speak just seconds before, she'd think her wife were dead. She couldn't see, but she could feel Jack's presence just a couple feet away, somewhere in the folds of hanging clothes. Holding her breath, she retreated into the bathroom and slid the pocket door closed.

"It's on the floor, babe. Not too much seasoning, just like you like it."

Again, not a word from the other side. Was Jack even aware of that noxious, poisonous *smell*? Like something had died and then crawled into its own asshole.

"Jack?"

She lowered herself to the bathroom floor, wanting to get on Jack's level. Wanting to feel some kind of connection. The soft scent of soap reached mercifully into her nostrils. She put her back to the pocket door and said her wife's name again.

Nothing.

Maybe she'd be more talkative after she'd eaten a little. Ash knew she had some flashlights in there she could use to eat by. But was she even aware that Ash had brought her food? Would she be able to smell the freshly fried chicken through that reek?

What *was* it? It couldn't be . . . her feet? The bandages on her heels?

"Jack, baby," she said, raising her voice. "I'm worried about you. I'm worried about your feet. I think you need medical attention or . . . it could get infected. I don't know, maybe it already is, it's been so long, but . . ."

Something moved on the other side of the door. She turned her head, pressing her ear to the cheap wood to hear better. Clinking. The utensils. Metal on ceramic. She breathed better, breathed in the soap and the strong cleaning supplies of the bathroom, already forgetting the pure strength of that overpowering smell that had hit her in the closet.

As she listened to Jack eat, she talked to the door. Focused on trivial things, funny things, like her "quarantine miracle" and finding her copy of *The Stand* and scouring it for "apocalypse pointers, ha-ha." Avoided heavier topics, like Jack's isolation and mental decay, like Mo's murder, like their dwindling food supplies, the majority of which Jack was eating right now.

Jack never responded, but that was okay. Ash could hear her scarfing away, meticulously cutting into the chicken and sucking it from the bone the way she did to gross out Ash at the dinner table. The sounds made her smile and think of a simpler time, a happier time, when they truly felt like partners.

There came a lull in their one-sided conversation. Through the door, the eating sounds had trickled down, and Ash wasn't sure if she was just imagining it, but she felt a *presence* just on the other side. She could imagine Jack, chicken grease still on her fingers, crawling from her clothing cocoon and pressing her back against the pocket door, just like Ash was doing, and now the two of them were sitting together with just a few inches of space between them.

With her foot, she flicked open the cabinet beneath the bathroom sink. She couldn't see it in the dark, but she knew where it was after her hunt for the scissors: there, hiding between the pipes like a gremlin, sat the first-aid kit. She leaned forward, snatched it up, and came back to rest against the door.

She steeled herself. *You can do this.*

"Jack, baby," she said, "you need help. I can help you. Can I . . . can I come inside? You don't have to leave the closet, I know you feel safe in there, but . . . I have fresh bandages here, and I really think I need to—"

"Yes."

Relief washed over Ash. "Yes? I can come in?"

Jack's voice, low, just past the wood of the door: "Yes. I want you."

Almost sobbing with relief, Ash climbed to her feet.

And slid the door open to her wife.

WHEN THE CARDIGAN MAN powered down the computer and everything went black, a strange thing happened. Jack was suddenly sure—absolutely certain, *one hundred percent convinced*—that what sat in the chair in front of her mom's old kitchen desk was changing . . . mutating.

It wasn't Morgan Kiner.

It wasn't the Cardigan Man.

It wasn't Ash.

It was a shark.

It was a shark, Jack *knew* it was a shark, its rubbery hide just inches from her hitched breath. It was sitting in the chair like a man, and its torso opened up like a vase of flowers but what was waiting for her wasn't roses or daisies but row after row of jagged, razor teeth. It was grinning at her in the dark just as the Cardigan Man always grinned at her, she knew it, she *knew*, and if she didn't get away fast she'd live the rest of her life as a thumbnail image on Morgan Kiner's computer screen.

She lunged away from that corner of the room, squirming across the mattress, and for a heart-stopping moment she was tangled in the bedspread and the shark was going to catch her, it was going to chomp onto the bed and shred it to bits until it reached her and then she'd go down its gullet like a ripe tomato in a wood chipper.

And then she was free and falling to the floor on the other side, the mattress safely between her and the desk and computer and shark, and then . . . and then, just as she had been positive that there was a shark in the bedroom, now she knew she was alone again. Nobody but her. The shark had swum away. Maybe it picked up Morgan Kiner's scent and went after her. Maybe it heard her loud swearing and went to punish her for her sins.

After an interminable time catching her breath, Jack crawled the few feet to the closet and closed the door behind her. She needed quiet; she needed absolute solitude. She wrapped herself in her cocoon and breathed heavily into the fabrics.

A knock came from the other end of the closet, speeding her heart back up. From the pocket door leading to the bathroom. Who was it now?

"What do you want," she said, squeezing her eyes shut.

"I brought something to eat. Open up and I'll feed it to you."

She'd know that voice anywhere.

It was the Cardigan Man.

She pressed her face into a hanging coat, breathing in the scratchy wool, and said into the fabric, "Where's Ash." Again, not a question—because a part of her didn't want to know . . . a part of her already knew.

The door slid open a crack. "She took off, Jackie boy."

Jack stifled a moan into the coat. She knew this would happen. In the end, it didn't take a bigoted neighbor or murderous landlord or hungry shark or deadly pandemic. In the end, Ash left because she thought her wife was crazy. She left because of Jack.

She heard the door slide open further and then a soft *clink* of cutlery as something was set down just outside her clothing cocoon. Food? She couldn't smell anything.

The door slid closed again and the Cardigan Man, returned to the bathroom, said, "It's on the floor, Jackie boy. My peace offering. Shark meat."

Her stomach grumbled. When was the last time she ate? She couldn't remember, but even the mention of food shot a searing pain into her jaw, and it salivated so much that she had to wipe drool away with the coat.

But she couldn't accept food from *him*, could she?

He'd been terrorizing her for months. He was the reason Ash had finally given up and left her. If he hadn't gotten inside Jack's head, if he hadn't stalked her and assaulted her, she and Ash could have spent this quarantine perfectly fine, maybe even coming out on the other side of it closer and more like they used to be.

And now he sounded . . . nice. Kind, even. It unsettled her. It made her feel off balance.

Or maybe that was the hunger speaking.

"Jackie boy," he said, and she could tell from the sound of his voice that he was sitting on the bathroom linoleum now. "I can't stop thinking about you . . . thinking about your *body*. Ash never could give you what I want to give you, Jackie boy, if you'd only let me. You should have heard the things she said about you on her way out . . ."

She couldn't wait any longer. Her heart thudding, she climbed from the cover of the clothes and groped for the plate of food. Her hand brushed a utensil, and it gave its tell-tale *clink*. She felt the metal tentatively: a fork . . . and a knife. She snatched the plate, the utensils falling to the carpet unheeded, and brought it back to the safety of her cocoon, and *now* she could smell it: rich, tasty *shark* meat. She brought it to her mouth with her hands, took a big bite, and moaned with pleasure.

As she ate, the Cardigan Man talked. She wasn't sure what about, she was so focused on the meat in her hands, but his voice sounded pleasant enough. She finished the food, not bothering to wipe the gristle and grease from her mouth or fingers, and crawled out of her cocoon again.

He'd stopped talking. She pressed her face to the pocket door, sliding a little from the shark grease, and held her breath, listening.

Then he spoke:

"Jackie boy . . . you need me. I *want* you. Can I come inside you? Don't even leave the closet, we can fuck on the floor. I know you want me, and clearly Ash—"

"Yes."

Something had changed in her body as she listened to him speak to her through the door. A flush from her lips all the way to her core. She groped her body in the dark and felt . . . free. Ash was no longer here to *judge* her, to tell her she was *crazy* and she *needed help*. Now it was just her and this man who had stripped away all her inhibitions, who had seen to her creamy center and looked the worst parts of her straight in the eye and said, *I want you.*

"Yes," he said. "I'm coming in."

"Yes," she said. One hand pinched her erect nipple, hard, eliciting a barely audible gasp from her lips; the other hand felt down along her leg and then pressed itself into her bandaged wound and it was a savage delight. "I want you."

And if this turned out to be a trick? If the Cardigan Man wasn't here to make desperate, carnal love to her? Well . . . she reached out across the carpet and felt her fingers close around the handle of the knife. She'd be ready for that, too.

The door slid open.

15

ASHLEY &
JACQUELINE

"Church Pastors Across Nation Open Doors in
Defiance of Coronavirus, to Devastating Results"
—*The Huffington Post*
June 2020

This whole anti-masker movement is strange to
me. Do these people refuse to wear seatbelts
too? Because that's basically what they're turning the U.S. into, just one giant car crash.
#Murica #FreedomIntensifies
@NotJustAnotherSheep69
12:31 PM · June 4, 2020
2.6K RTs 33.3K likes

ASH STEPPED INTO THE CLOSET, holding her breath.

The shift in darkness was subtle, but still there: Ash
had left the bathroom door open as she spoke through
the pocket door, and what little natural light that fell
through the sliding-door window and reached the

bathroom was now completely gone as she slid the pocket door closed behind her. The memory of the bathroom's smell and that of the now-devoured chicken thighs edged out the worst of that dead-animal reek, but Ash was still careful to take shallow breaths.

In the pitch black, she felt Jack kneeling before her. Soft whispers reached her ears, of cotton on skin . . . Jack wasn't removing her panties, was she? No, that was ridiculous. Pajama bottoms, maybe, so Ash could have better access to the bandages at her feet.

Something touched her stomach: greasy fingers, a single hand, tickling that stretch of skin below her belly button. Ash jumped and stifled a cry of alarm, working to turn it into a giggle.

Jack whispered, "I can feel you so hard already."

Ash paused. Had she heard that right?

She cleared her throat, still careful not to breathe in too deeply. "I brought the first-aid kit," she said, holding up the plastic box. She felt stupid, like a kindergartner showing her *Goosebumps* lunch box to the class because she'd forgotten it was her turn for show and tell.

Jack laughed throatily in the dark. "No, we don't need a condom. I want to *feel* you."

Ash's blood ran cold. She'd *definitely* heard that. "What the *fuck* are you talking about?"

But Jack didn't seem to understand just how angry and confused she'd made Ash. That one greasy hand tickled down Ash's belly and fumbled with her jeans, tugging and popping the buttons. "Oh, you wanna play rough?"

With her free hand, Ash clutched Jack's wrist in a viselike grip. "Jack, stop. Fucking *stop*."

And Jack giggled. She *giggled*. She sounded like a

fucking loon.

A voice in Ash's head chanted like children on a play-ground: *You did this to her, Ash. You shouldn't have left her by herself all this time. It's your fault,* your *fault,* YOOOOUR FAAAAAAULT—

Jack tried to wrench her hand away, still laughing duskily, sounding absolutely certifiable. But Ash held on. Not caring, Jack lunged forward, darting her head toward Ash like a snapping turtle, like a shark. She caught Ash's loosened jeans in her teeth, still laughing around the metal studded buttons in her mouth, and yanked down.

"Jack, what—"

"C'mon—"

Ash bucked her hips, yanking the jeans from Jack's mouth. A button pinged away—or maybe it was one of Jack's teeth. It was impossible to tell in the dark.

"—show me that cock, show me how much you want me—"

Ash dropped the first-aid kit and slapped Jack hard across the face.

Everything stopped, and Ash gasped, horrified at what she'd done. But it was that word—*cock*—it had just surprised it out of her, sent her hand whipping out in the dark. There was a part of her that knew what she was do-ing as she struck out, and it was calculating, controlling; it knew that the fastest way to stop this nonsense was to knock some sense into Jack. This part of Ash scared her. It was her father.

"Jack, ohmygod, I'm so sorry . . ."

But the damage had been done, Ash knew. She couldn't have done worse even if she'd found the knife on the discarded plate of chicken bones and stabbed Jack in the heart. They'd never gotten physical with each other, not like this, and they'd both confided in the other about what that constant threat of violence hovering over their childhood homes had done to their anxieties, their fears.

Jack was silent, seemingly knocked out of her play-acting.

"Say something, Jack," Ash gasped, and now she was breathing heavily, and that dead smell hit her in the face like she'd hit Jack.

That small part of her, the part that was her father, that knew exactly what a smack across the face would mean, felt . . . triumphant. She was *glad* she'd done it, if only because she was afraid that she didn't know what had been going through Jack's head. She didn't know if Jack was just goofing around or if she was actually hallucinating someone other than her wife coming inside the dark of the closet.

"You hit me," Jack finally said. Her voice was barely audible.

A lump climbed Ashley's throat, choking her with tears.

"You hit me," Jack said again.

Ash dropped to her knees, now on Jack's level. "Yes, and I shouldn't have, I never will again, I'm so sorry, I . . ."

She stopped. Jack's words finally sank into her brain, like tenterhooks. She'd misheard her. Jack hadn't said, *You hit me.*

She'd said . . . *Yes, hit me.*

Ash's mind reeled: *What . . . the . . . FUCK?!*

"Harder," Jack said, "give it to me harder—"

"ENOUGH!"

Ash was panting now, spots dancing in her vision, maybe from the reek of Jack's feet or from the shock of finding her wife like this. She grabbed Jack by the shoulders and shook her. Jack didn't shy away, but seemed to lean into it, like she was enjoying it. *Harder,* she'd said, and who the fuck did she think she was talking to?

"*Enough,* Jack! Enough of this shit. What is *wrong* with you?"

She shook her again, and now she noticed how skinny Jack was, how weak, how she flailed like a ragdoll.

"It's *me*, it's *Ashley*, it's your *wife*. I came in here to *help* you. I brought bandages for your feet!"

It was too dark to tell, but after staring into pitch black for so long Ash felt like her eyes could pick out shapes now, and she thought maybe she could detect a change of expression come over Jack's face.

"Stop," Jack said, her voice weak. "It's not fun for me anymore."

Ash still held her firmly by the shoulders. "That's what I'm trying to tell you, babe. It's not fun for me either. It stopped being fun a long fucking time ago. Let me help you."

"Let me go, you bastard," Jack breathed. "You . . ." But her voice trailed off.

Ash released her grip on Jack's shoulders. "I'm sorry. I'm—" She choked back a sob. "I'm so sorry, b-baby, I didn't mean to hit you, I didn't want to, I—" She stopped, gathering herself. "Will you grab one of the flashlights for me? I don't know where you keep them, but we need some light, we . . ."

As she fumbled on the carpet for the dropped first-aid kit, she felt Jack lean down to one side—to grab a nearby flashlight, presumably. And then Jack spoke, and again, her words made no sense.

"You bastard, you drove her out. You made her leave me."

"What . . . ?" Ash's fingers paused at one corner of the first-aid kit.

"I'll kill you."

Something rushed at Ash out of the darkness. For a split second, Ash thought it must be Jack's open palm, returning the slap across the face, tit for tat, and she was almost relieved, almost *wanted* it to happen, to feel better for hurting Jack—

But that calculating, controlling voice, the voice that reminded her of her father, said, *You better keep your guard up, Ashley,* and something about the way Jack's almost imperceptible silhouette rose up sent klaxons blaring through her head. Her fingers left the first-aid kit, still lying on the carpet, and she brought her hand up to shield her face, thinking, *Surely you're being silly, Ash, surely Jack would never—*

The knife plunged into the center of her palm and out the other end.

Ash was too shocked to scream; she grunted from the force of Jack's hand coming down on her. Now Jack was pressing both hands against the handle of the blade, slippery with grease and now blood, and Ash brought her other hand up, too, and shoved her free palm into Jack's chest.

Jack fell away, the knife slipping from her grip.

It was still so goddamn dark. Ash wasn't sure if *she* was the one hallucinating now, or if her eyesight had adjusted to the blackness. But she swore she could see the knife still jutting out from the center of her hand, like a mutant sixth finger. It quivered there like an arrow after spearing the bull's-eye.

Finally her voice caught up to her and she screamed.

Still screaming—or maybe not, maybe that was the klaxon still in her head, she was beyond knowing for sure—with her other hand she grasped the greasy knife handle and pulled its blade from her palm. She felt more than heard the blade's serrated edge saw across muscle and bone and tendon and skin.

A light clicked on, seemingly miles away, like a lighthouse spotlight piercing the fog blanketing her screaming pain. It strobed out from behind a wall of hanging clothes and then found her, settling on her face, blinding her.

She'd come in here with a peace offering.

She'd come in here to dress Jack's wounds.

She'd come in here to have the hard conversations.

To fix their marriage.

And instead—

Instead, Jack had stabbed her with a knife.

Ash took in a deep breath of the death reek, now mingled with a coppery blood tang, and screamed:

"I WANT A DIVORCE!"

JACK DROPPED THE FLASHLIGHT. It spun away on the carpet. Moments before, it had illuminated not the face of the Cardigan Man, not his gasmask or hockey mask or neatly trimmed beard or even his grinning skull . . . but the face of her wife. Of Ashley.

Her eyes, bulging, reflected the flashlight. And she'd screamed . . .

She'd screamed a word that had pierced through all of the Cardigan Man's tricks. Jack had been wrong—it wasn't him coming in here to ravage her . . . and Ash hadn't left her. She should have known that her wife would never leave her.

That is, until Ash said the D word.

Until now.

IV

GROWS

16

JACQUELINE & ASHLEY

"When China first bunkered down under a government-mandated quarantine to wait out the novel coronavirus, Chinese officials were hoping for a baby boom as a direct result of forced close quarters. Population growth has been at an all-time low, and the one-child mandate was lifted in light of recent events. However, it seems COVID-19 had the exact opposite in mind: it isn't pregnancy that has gone viral, but divorce. Couples are emerging from quarantine practically begging attorneys to put an end to their marital bliss. This reporter suggests that this uptick in divorce—a 600% surge in divorce rates from last year, no less—might act as a warning to the rest of the world."

—*Forbes* article
April 2020

THIS WAS THE ONLY PLACE Jack felt safe these days: the loam folding over her like a downy comforter, like when her mother would come in at night and tuck her in, snug and safe—except this time her dad wouldn't come in shortly after her mom left and plant a whiskey-sharp kiss on her, with her tucked in so tight that she couldn't raise her hands to push him off. The loam kept all of that at bay, kept her snug and safe in its womb. It was even better than her closet cocoon, though she hadn't visited there since the incident, since the D word. Here, in her loam-filled coffin, she was safe from all that. Here, in the dark of the earth, she could hide from the fear. Down here there was no pandemic. No panicky world powers twitching over the nuclear launch codes. No rush to the grocery store or unemployment. No wife calling her paranoid. None of that. Just her, this coffin bed of fertilizer, and the alien sludge. The sludge was the only thing that had been able to seep inside through the splintery cracks in the coffin. The battery-acid taste was gone from her throat—that had just been the taste of fear, not the sludge, and now the fear was gone, the fear couldn't reach her in here—and she realized, shame-faced and blushing like a child, that the sludge didn't want to choke her. It didn't want to climb past her lips and drip down her esophagus. It wanted to mother her, nurture her, wanted to tuck her in, safe and snug. It wanted to let in the dirt and loam and seedlings. It wanted to tend to her wounds and help her to transform into a new Jacqueline. The sludge first seeped over her feet and into her bandages; it brought a pleasant numbing agent that put a lid on the constant singing live wire that was the pain in her heels. From there it slithered up her calves and thighs and pooled in her belly button and the slight indent between and below her breasts. It coated her entire body until her limbs and lips hummed and tingled. It was Novocain, and she was getting her wisdom teeth pulled, and she wondered if the alien sludge was surgically removing something else from her. But no—if it was removing anything, it was the fear; it was the pain. It was Ash. It wasn't here to *remove*. It was here to . . . to what? To *grow*? Yes, that felt right. It was a friend, if only because it did not need to understand her to coexist. It spread across her body like an embalming paste and slowly sucked her skin dry so that her pores gawped wide in desperate thirst, and all the meal worms and potato bugs squirmed in the dirt until they covered her and her friend and it all fermented into mulch. She would wake from pleasant dreams to find that she could feel new appendages sprouting from her body, nubs of cartilage questing up into the earth. She would smile and drink some of the loam into her gullet. In her dreams, so pleasant and calm, her friend the alien sludge—no longer *alien*, now it was *home*—would whisper to her of what it was doing, what it was helping her to become. And as it whispered, she was aware of it on her sleeping body, still coating every inch of her skin's surface, and seeping into the pores, and decorticating her so she would resemble one of those skinless bodies of squirming muscle and nerve from anatomy class. Coring her out like an apple. She would wake up again and find more new parts of her grown from her body, or perhaps grafted on. After some time, she didn't know how long, maybe a month, maybe eons drifting in the cosmic aether, she opened her eyes and found that she could see in her coffin bed. The loam had been pulled down to her collar bone like that selfsame comforter from childhood. She looked down at her body. It was glowing. Soft oranges and ambers and yellows spread across the small space of her coffin. They were her. Her new body had flowered in the loam, poking mushroom heads and stalks through the bed of dirt. Buds shed petals in quick succession like a time-lapsed shot in a nature show. Her body continued to germinate and sprout and bud, from her daddy's little girl to what she was becoming. A garden. She felt . . . *whole*. A mycelial network spread throughout her body like a warm fizzy drink on Christmas morning. She was a garden, yes, a *forest*. So plentiful, full-bodied like an aged Merlot, sprouting up until mushroom heads and flowering buds *thunked* against the coffin's ceiling and crowded it and pushed and the coffin split open like a pharaoh's desecrated sarcophagus. Her friend was still with her, was now one with her, tamping down her fear and saying, *It's okay, break free of your grave, we're strong enough now,* and she found that it was true. She pushed the soil and splintered planks of wood away from her as easily as an untucked comforter, and she climbed from her coffin bed and sat up. It was still dark in the bedroom, a forever darkness since Doug had shut them from the rest of the decayed world. She opened her eyes as wide as they could, trying to cut through the black. There, lying next to her, was a man. He, too, was just waking. No longer in his cardigan, his gasmask removed the night before. A line of thick hair ran down his chest like a strip of carpet. She wanted to press her nose to it and inhale. He blinked up at her, yawned, and grinned.

"Good morning, Jackie boy," he said. "Sleep well?"

"Like a dream," she said, and kissed him.

* * *

ASH FEASTED ON A MOUSE.

It was almost laughable to call such a small thing a "feast," but she stifled the giggles rising in her throat. If she started laughing now, she was afraid she wouldn't be able to stop until she laughed so much she threw up. And she couldn't afford to upchuck a single piece of food. Not these days.

It sickened her how much she was drooling over this poor little mouse. Even before she'd cooked it, when it was scurrying around, just as afraid of her as she might have been of it before the apocalypse, her mouth had started salivating as she'd chased it through the apartment. But beggars couldn't be choosers—though if she *could*, she would have chosen a rat over a mouse. More meat.

Eating it now, she couldn't help but think back to a much simpler time, in the second or third grade, when her entire class had dissected owl pellets. The goal was to reconstruct the entire skeleton of a mouse and glue all the little bones onto their corresponding spots on the placemat with the mouse skeleton diagram. But little seven- or eight-year-old Ashley refused to be fooled. How could they *know* these bones were all from the same mouse? They *couldn't*. Wasn't it more likely that Ashley and her classmates were all piecing together little mouse Frankensteins? Young Ashley had never seen the movie or even heard of Frankenstein's monster (not yet), but she was smart enough to imagine the concept: a tibia and fibula from Mommy Mouse, radius and ulna from Daddy Mouse, sacrum from Uncle Mouse, mandibles from little Johnny Mouse, and littlest Sally Mouse's entire vertebral column, all ripped from each family member to be glued together for all of eternity. She'd demanded that her teachers allow her to assign each bone its own identity, with little stats like baseball cards—*Baby Mouse, 6 weeks old, favorite color is yellow, wanted to grow up to be a mouse doctor*—and then she'd held her own private funeral service in her backyard later that day, covering the completed placemat of mouse bones with a thin but serviceable layer of dirt and using respectably straight twigs to form a cross atop the mound.

Had that really been a *simpler* time?

Well . . . yes.

Take today, for instance. Ash was sitting on her yoga mat, in a tank top and sweatshorts that needed a wash six weeks ago. Completely alone and shut off from the world. Unable to call her mom and say, "Hey, remember that time you got a call from the school about my owl pellet project? Did Dad ever find it buried in the backyard?" Unable to call anyone. Unable to do anything but gaze out this sliding-door window at the beautiful trees and hillside and river and feel herself wither away to nothing.

The sunlight streaming through the window did little to penetrate the gloom just half a dozen paces inside the apartment. What light did reach its spindly fingers inside shone on silver pots and plastic bowls and glass cups and the crock pot some relative of Ash's had gifted them at their wedding. Dozens of containers—just about every single one she could find in the kitchen—scattered around tabletops and shelves and the floor.

Weeks ago, Ash had woken from a dead sleep with the sudden surety that Doug, *fucking* Doug, would shut off the water for good any day now. It was an unsolvable mystery as to why he hadn't done so in the beginning of all this madness. What, he could sign their death warrants but thought it was too heartless to add dehydration to the list of causes of death?

This had been the night after her final fight with Jack ("I WANT A DIVORCE!" echoing in her head, *that* was actually what had woken her), so one hand was all she had to open the cupboards and gather every receptable she could find. She had to turn on the kitchen sink and leave it running as she lifted each cup and bowl and pot single-handed and held it under the faucet. She'd even gone and filled the bathtub full of water, though she hoped she'd never have to use it—who knew what Jack might decide to do with it, with her bandaged feet. And anyway, shouldn't Ash have a washing station somewhere to clean her own wound with?

The hand still stung, all these weeks later. She could use it to help her other hand bring the cooked mouse meat to her mouth, but it wasn't easy. It was swaddled in gauze. She had no idea how long these things took to heal—if it *was* healing. But it hurt like a motherfucker, like nothing she'd gone through before, and she had a sneaking suspicion that all the little bones and bits that made up the circuit board of her hand weren't mending back together without proper medical care. What was she supposed to do? It wasn't like she could google it.

A part of her felt a strange sense of power in being cut from everything she once relied on. No phone, no electricity, no internet, no access to the outside world whatsoever . . . just her and her ability to survive on her own. It brought back a savage sense of independence, of control, that she hadn't known she'd lost.

The mouse, for instance. Here she was eating a meal

she'd caught, killed, skinned, cooked, and seasoned all by herself. You couldn't buy *this* from your local H-E-B market. She had a good idea that it wouldn't have been tasty back when she could be choosey about her diet, but now it tasted like a Thanksgiving turkey. Now, sitting before the huge window on the second story of this prison, she could take a chunk of meat from the mouse's skeleton and look out on the wilderness and imagine it as her kingdom.

She'd found the mouse in the rice. She'd been carefully rationing the one and only grocery delivery from before fucking Doug had soldered their door shut, and this morning she'd approached the pantry thinking, *Just two more days of rice . . . and then it's all empty, Ash.* But in the pantry, when she'd lifted the lid from the container and shone the flashlight inside, she'd yelled at the sight of a little mouse scurrying around—around an *empty* rice bin.

"Motherfucker ate my rice!"

Before she could do anything but yell, the frightened mouse disappeared through a hole in the container—a bullet hole from Doug's gun-toting henchmen. She'd taped it shut, but now, thanks to that single bullet, her last rice was lining the stomach of Stuart Little.

"Fucking Doug!"

She'd grabbed the broom from the coat closet and chased the mouse around in hysterics, unsure what she'd do but sure that she fucking *hated* that mouse—thinking in a mad second that maybe she'd dig that errant bullet from the rock wall and force-feed it to the fucking thief . . . and then her mouth had started watering, and she knew what she had to do. She'd end up eating that final serving of rice anyway. In a manner of speaking.

Once she'd caught it (the broom had been just as

useless as always, and she'd chucked it across the couch, instead killing the mouse beneath her brick of a biology textbook, which had said *nothing* about how to treat a knife wound through the hand), she briefly wondered if she would have to eat the thing raw. She'd never dressed a turkey or deboned a fish or done any of those outdoorsy, Girl Scout activities as a kid. But the gas had been shut off with the water—no more pan-fried *anything*, chicken or mouse. She'd puzzled over this dilemma for a mere moment before shoving the antique chest to the side of the open living area and building a campfire in the middle of the goddamn apartment floor.

After a few wasted matches, it was clear to her that the stupid biology textbook's pages weren't quick to burn. Ah well, it had served its purpose. She quickly found another cardboard box shoved deep in the closet and cried out with delight when she saw its contents.

It was their wedding box.

A box carefully filled with memorabilia dedicated to their day of matrimony, a box which Ash had meticulously curated and Jack had studiously ignored. It was perfect.

She'd dragged it to the makeshift fire she'd already attempted and quickly coaxed flames first from their marriage certificate and then feeding the building flames countless congratulations cards from guests and left-over RSVPs and photographs and, finally, their vows.

It was deeply therapeutic, and it was one of the few times Ash actually allowed herself to think about that part of her life, about what she'd meant when she'd screamed "I WANT A DIVORCE!" to Jack all those weeks ago. All her thoughts on the matter still seemed to dance around the subject as she'd danced from guest to guest in the whirlwind of her own wedding; all her words of wisdom to herself oblique, trimmed at the edges so as to trick the eye.

Though she did not cry. She hadn't cried since that day.

The fire built, she distracted herself as she worked over the dead mouse with thoughts of making bone broth from the little fucker's remains. She distracted herself with jokes about how she must look to anyone outside who could see through the window: the fire glinted off the windowpane, shooting her reflection back at her, a grungy little scavenger hunched over a small fire, her gaunt features and shaved skull looking ghoulish yet delightedly alive in its amber glow, muttering to herself and chanting like her witch-coven neighbors. She suddenly missed those witches. She wondered if they'd escaped, or how they were faring if they hadn't. Had they gone full Donner Party yet?

She forced herself to scrutinize her reflection closer, longer. Even in the daytime gloom, the fire threw demonic shadows up across her face. She looked like a soldier. She'd kept her hair shorn close to the scalp, not out of any necessity but out of boredom, out of something to do, and out of her desire to keep a firm hold on her new identity, her Jackless self. Her Theseus's ship.

Yes, that's what she looked like: a soldier. Her face was hard, grim, dry. Beneath that, it was almost shocking how her body had transformed. She wasn't weak and shriveled away like she'd expected. Again with that new word she'd never thought to apply to herself: *hard*. Maybe she'd been hard the whole time, and she'd been shying away from such decidedly unfeminine imagery, but dammit that's what Ash was, she was hard, she was a soldier. Her body was cut into firm lines, the muscles pressing through the skin. She liked this reflection. She decided it wasn't the new Ashley, just the *real* one emerging under duress.

And now she sat on the yoga mat, the sweet smell of cooked meat cutting through her own body odor, and raised the stripped rodent carcass to the outside world in a toast.

"To the end of the world."

And she snapped its bones for marrow.

JACK, TOO, WAS HAVING HER FINAL MEAL.

She sat near the foot of her mattress, her legs dangling off the bed so her heels could hang in open space. The comforter was bunched around her and about her shoulders like a shawl.

"Open up, Jackie boy."

She leaned her head back, yawning her jaw wide and sticking out her tongue, going "Ahhhhh" like she'd done as a kid when the doctor put the popsicle stick down her throat. A dollop of something chalky and delicious plopped onto her tongue.

"Be sure to chew it thoroughly, Jackie boy. That's where all the nutrients are."

She nodded as she chewed, the flavors bursting in her mouth like effervescent fireworks.

The taste reminded her of something Morgan Kiner had done when they were kids: a whole sleeve of Mentos shoved down the throat of a two-liter Coca-Cola bottle. She'd been too scared to get closer than a dozen feet to it while Morgan set it up in her craggy dirt-clod-ridden backyard—not too scared of the chemical reaction it was supposed to cause, not too scared of the mouth of the Coke bottle launching through one of their eyeballs (*skull-fucking* them, Morgan had called it); no, she'd been scared of what her mother might say if she were caught doing such a thing. Being so destructive. Toying with *science*, which everyone knew was to blame for abortions and the homosexuals.

And here she was, not just setting the dominoes and running for cover, but igniting the chemical reaction *in her own mouth*. Between her teeth. She chewed, reveling in the live-wire taste, and grinned.

The Cardigan Man grinned back. "Want some more, Jackie boy?"

She swallowed, nodding. "All gone." She yawned her jaw wide and stuck her tongue out to prove it. "Ahhhhhh."

The Cardigan Man took another handful of the stuff. She watched him mix expired paints, oil and acrylic, with chunks of pastel. She watched him dip an hors d'oeuvre–sized chunk into a pile of glitter, like powdered sugar. She watched him raise it to her mouth, one hand cupped lovingly under the treat to catch any stray flakes of deliciousness, and place it upon her quivering tongue.

"Eat up, Jackie boy."

Jack grinned. She loved when he called her that.

It made her . . . *glow*.

17

ASHLEY & JACQUELINE

"Folks, how do we know the extent of Hillary Clinton's involvement in this virus spread? Has anyone—anyone willing to tell the truth, that is—actually taken the time to read through all those emails?"

—Glenn Beck
The Glenn Beck Program
mere moments before Alex Jones and a dozen of his supporters broke into Beck's in-home sound studio and decapitated him with the golden trumpet of a Moroni statuette, which fell from an LDS temple the previous morning in an earthquake and was immediately sold on eBay for $3 million

I CAN HEAR STRANGE SOUNDS coming from Jack's room.

Jack's room. Not <u>ours</u>. Not anymore.

Fuck.

Okay, fine, Diary, I'll write about what happened. And don't think I don't see the irony—me, Ashley, the one who spent the first twenty years of her literate life spilling her guts in ink to you, the one who has been asking for the last few years that her wife constantly talk through their issues with her, to not let anything fester, is now ignoring her problems. I haven't watched that particular pot in, what, three weeks? four?—is it July already?—and now the water's boiling.

And while I say I've been ignoring it, I think we both know that's a load of bullshit. Sure, on the surface, I'm ignoring my marriage problems like it's my job. (Remember those? Jobs?) But beneath the surface . . . down just under what I allow in the visible spectrum of my awareness, all this shit has been roiling and—well, that word again, festering. Does boiling water help with infections?

Now I'm mixing up my metaphors.

The truth is that these problems aren't new, and neither are they all Jack's fault.

The truth is, we've become codependent as fuck—not something that happens overnight, and not something you can blame on just one single dependent.

The truth is, that word, "divorce," has been down in that roiling subsurface for a while now. At least a year. Probably more. And moving to a new city was never going to just fix us.

The hardest TRUTH of all, with a capital T-R-U-T-H, Diary, is the real whopper, the one I've been building up the courage to write . . . and that's how I've handled—or, rather, not handled—my wife's struggle with mental illness.

Mental illness. Did it really take all this time for me to say the words, even just in writing? Instead, I've been using placeholder words, like paranoid and trauma and—I'm ashamed to say it—crazy. The closest I've come to naming the elephant in the room is the oh-so-helpful "You need help," never elaborated on or followed through with and always used as ammunition in a fight.

If I truly meant my vows, wouldn't I have done something? Gone to the doctor with her, or called and interviewed psychologists or therapists, or even suggested some kind of holistic-medicine bullshit? I'm not saying I didn't love Jack, Diary. I did—I still do. But burning my vows yesterday . . .

(Yeah, I burned my vows. I also ate a mouse, so that's a thing.)

Burning my vows felt . . . freeing.

It felt like a first step toward treating that festering wound.

Begs the question: What's the next step?

JACK UNWRAPPED HER FOOT in the light of the glow.

It was *her* glow, and hers only. She cultivated it and coaxed it from her body like a particularly stubborn plot of bamboo—at first shy, unwilling to flower and to fruit; but then, she felt a gardener's sense of sweaty pride as it rolled off her body in waves, glowing exponentially brighter until she felt like a red giant in an impossibly vast swatch of empty cosmic black. An amber aura wreathed her body with its glow like a fine mist. She loved her aura.

Somewhere in the night, the Cardigan Man had snuggled up to her within her aura and gently reminded her that she was wounded. That if she didn't take care of her body, mightn't the aura go away? That thought had chased itself in her head all night, like an ouroboros, *the aura will leave you the aura will leave you she will leave you too she will*, until she crawled from her mycelial grave determined to finally unbandage her feet.

The Cardigan Man was pressed lovingly—covetously—against her. She could feel the swell of his manhood along the base of her spine, his breath feathering her nape. His arms wrapped around her, one hand resting between her thighs, the other under her breasts. He whispered into her ear step-by-step instructions as she attended the bandages.

The first step was to find where the ACE bandage ended, so she could unwrap it. She'd thought this would be made possible by the light of her aura, but after, what, two, three months?, she couldn't distinguish one layer of the bandage from another; it was just one continuous swath. She noticed with distant alarm that the bandage didn't feel all that different beneath her fingertips from the skin surrounding it.

Once she *did* find the end of the bandage, carefully sussed from the other layers with one long fingernail, the next step was to unwind it, layer after layer. Like an onion. And, just like an onion, the smell that escaped from beneath each layer hit her with a force that squeezed tears from her eyes. She could taste it on her tongue.

After the overpowering smell came a tug.

She paused. The bandage hadn't unraveled all its layers, yet it seemed suddenly reluctant to come undone. She pulled harder. And yelled in pain.

"Fuck!"

"Breathe, Jackie boy," the Cardigan Man said, pressing her naked body tighter against his.

But she was only dimly aware of him now because the *pain*—

"Just rip it off," he whispered. "Like a band-aid."

She nodded, biting her lip to stem the tears, and tugged harder. The bandage stretched to the edge of its elastic limits, the whole time her skin feeling as though it had gotten itself snagged on a fishhook and it was being yanked from the bone.

She stopped, her breath hissing out of her in sharp gasps.

"I can't do it," she said, breathing heavily.

"Shhh," the Cardigan Man said, his breath hot on her ear. "Of course you can, Jackie boy."

As he squeezed her tighter, she leaned into him and opened her mouth. His hand cinched around her, spreading her thighs enough so that his fingers played notes against her crotch, and she gasped, her breath shuddering from the tears. His fingers massaged her down there, like she used to do when she was a girl and she thought Jesus wasn't looking. His other hand turned its palm toward her and cupped her left breast, his fingers slowly making their way to the nipple and pinching and teasing.

And he whispered, "Shhh, baby . . ."

And she moaned.

And he whispered, "Try again, babe."

And her moans rose and swelled in shouts as he entered her and she screamed in orgasm, and as she screamed her hands convulsed inward, clutching his arms about her sweaty body with its glow. The bandage, still in her clutching hand, pulled with her. A tearing sound, like

Velcro, a barely audible undercurrent to her own shouts and screams and moans, but she was only vaguely aware of this or what it might be because she was twisting in his arms, twisting in climax.

"Shhh," he said again, and again she screamed and pulled.

MORE SCREAMS FROM JACK'S ROOM, Diary.

Not all of them sound like Jacqueline, either.

What the fuck is going on in there?

That's just another way I've failed my wife. Become codependent? Check. Ignore signs of the need for professional help? Check. Then, after all that, sit out here and let your wife starve to death or die of sepsis? Check and check.

I stopped trying to bring her meals a long time ago. What could she possibly be eating in there? I haven't checked the water levels in the bathtub, but I suppose if she's still alive to make all those strange noises right now she must be at least drinking water.

I read enough of that biology textbook, before trying (and failing) to burn it, to send a whole lot of high school knowledge rushing back to twenty-eight-year-old Ashley—all that knowledge sixteen-year-old Ashley thought would be useless in her adult life. Funny, right? Yeah. Fucking hilarious.

Anyway, I remembered a rant my old science teacher went on . . . or was it phys. ed.? I don't actually remember, but then, my brain isn't really firing on all cylinders at the moment. Starvation and all that.

The rant was about the essential vitamins our

bodies need. About the things that start to break down when we don't keep up our levels of vitamin C, vitamin K, amino acids, calcium . . . apparently our bodies go full cannibal when trapped in a corner like this. Like, at a cellular level or something. Our bodies will leech calcium from our own bones or shed hair like a chemo patient, stop regenerating skin cells or run our blood too thin to coagulate, give us scurvy.

Jaws ain't got nothin' on THAT horror movie.

I think I can feel some of that in my body. I mean, I've been making sure to drink water regularly, but food? This place is pretty much stripped like a carcass. Does that make me a vulture?

More screams . . . and these are weird, Diary. They're . . . guttural? But also kind of lusty, like she's filming hardcore porn in there or something.

My heart's racing. I'm actually <u>scared</u> of whatever's happening in there. But it's that old *Jaws* nugget: everyone fears what they cannot see.

Maybe that's why I'm afraid of my future.

I can't see it.

. . .

JESUS H. CHRIST.

She just howled, fucking HOWLED, like a fucking werewolf, and I mean <u>really</u> like a werewolf, like if I opened that door right now I'd find that my wife's gone, that she's . . . <u>transformed</u> . . . changed into some inhuman thing, some beast, some monster. She already stabbed my hand with a knife, but now that I'm leaving her . . .

What would the thing inside that bedroom do to me?

* * *

THE BANDAGE WAS FINALLY OFF Jack's right foot, and
with it some of her skin.

Jack's best guess was that somehow the new skin had
grafted onto or grown into the nonstick gauze. She
thought maybe she'd read something about skin regener-
ation (or maybe Ash had told her about it?) about how
the average person's skin grew back completely in three
weeks' time. She'd wrapped these wounds and then basically ignored them long enough for new skin to grow
back nearly five times over.

So much for "nonstick" . . .

All the sweat and heat had flushed from her body,
and the Cardigan Man was now nowhere to be seen. Figured—there for the pain, gone for the consequences.
Without his naked body wrapped around hers, Jack suddenly felt cold. Her glow had lost its luster, and now that
amber aura shone a sickly pus-yellow. Flashes of her time
in the bathroom all those months ago, poking and stabbing and cutting that throbbing, tumorous sac from her
foot and waiting for countless wriggling spiders to come
pouring from the gelatinous boil, razor-sharp legs ticking
up the stubble of her leg, searching for another hole to
climb into—

She shook the thought away. That's *not* what happened. Nothing had come screaming out of her wound
except for that gross discharge, and that had been more
of a *squish* than a scream. Nothing had come out of her
then, and nothing would come out of her now.

Right? her mind asked. It was suddenly unsure.

Her hands quested forward in the diminished glow,
whispering her trembling fingers along her right leg, leaving a trail of gooseflesh in their wake. She reached her

ankle, her leg now scooted up, the knobby knee pressed painfully into her boob and ribs. She was vaguely aware of and revolted by the way her body, now not much more than skin and bones, just folded up like a connector set; it reminded her of those metal folding chairs from her parents' church, the ones that were always cold and always pressed into your body painfully.

When she reached the recently unwrapped part of her foot, her fingers paused. The smell was overpowering, like rancid cheese, but the pain . . . the pain had retreated from her mind just like the Cardigan Man; the pain had been conspicuously absent in the afterglow of that terrible bandage-and-skin-tearing-away shock.

She plunged forward, digging her knee deeper into her ribcage, and felt . . .

What *was* that?

She wished she could control her new glow, wished she could will it into a brighter illumination to see by. Her foot was now swathed in shadows. Again, that image of spiders—the shadows resolving themselves into an army of skittering arachnids, pouncing on her and devouring her and nesting in her remains. She forced herself to shove it away.

She sank her fingers into the tissue where the wound used to be—

And gasped.

In the gloom, it took her some moments to process what she felt at her fingertips. There was the torn skin that had been disturbed from the bandage and nonstick gauze being ripped away. There was some weird substance that flaked away—dried skin, she supposed, or maybe (*gag*) more of that pus discharge, dried or fermented into some kind of chalky paste not unlike the art supplies she and the Cardigan Man had taken to snacking on. But as she began to massage her ankle and heel so that the dead skin and other bits sloughed off and fell away, she felt—

"What *is* that?" she said aloud.

The Cardigan Man wasn't there to tell her.

Folds of something altogether different from her skin but still attached to it. As she felt whatever it was and massaged it from beneath the torn new skin of her foot, she tried to pinpoint what it reminded her of. Waxen yet impossibly soft . . . pliable . . . like . . .

"Flowers," she whispered.

That was it. They were petals, coming apart under her fingers as if opening up to her touch. Baby-soft, like nothing she'd ever felt before, and could they be growing out of *her*? Tears fell down her cheeks and pattered on the bedspread like raindrops.

Delicately, she cupped one bud—for there was more than one, maybe three or four in total—that had peeked its head out of the back of her ankle like a spur. She cupped it in her palms and coaxed its petals apart like the shy wings of a butterfly, and from its mouth came a spark, like an ember, floating dreamily upward as if on a balmy draft on a lazy afternoon.

The ember hovered before her, and she'd never felt so much love in her life.

THE NOISES HAVE STOPPED, Diary. And I'm relieved. They could have stopped because she's dead, because her body gave in to starvation or infection or any number of things—maybe even suicide, maybe she thought of how her wife is leaving her and dragged those horrible scissors down the inside of her forearm—and yet here I am, relieved I don't have to listen to her anymore.

Whatever's happened in there, the silence is a relief.

God, I sound horrible. I think I'm in shock.

Did I tell you I've packed, Diary?

Don't worry, I'm taking you with me.

I didn't pack for the longest time. Couldn't. Every time I considered preparing and planning a trip out of this deathtrap, all I could hear was that thundering gunfire that took Mo's life. What if they're still waiting out there?

Yeah, the possibility of guns is what I think of now—not my wife. I guess I've finally made peace with the idea that I'm leaving her . . .

But anyway, I figured even fucking Doug couldn't manage to guard this place for that long. It's been weeks since Mo was shot. In fact, Doug and his goons probably split back when he cut the water supply.

So I've packed. It's not one of those big backpacks that hikers use, but it'll have to hold everything I want to take. I have no idea what's waiting for me out there, so the less I haul out with me the easier I can move.

No food—not a single morsel of that to be found in here, not even a mouse—but a couple sealed bottles of water. The first-aid kit. A flashlight. Fresh clothes (well, not fresh, but not as stinking as the others; also found in that closet with the box of books and journals and the wedding box). Aspirin. Mouthwash. A few tampons, though I haven't had my period in a while (silver lining of starvation?). My old novels and notebooks.

I know paper is an unnecessary weight, but . . . it's an old part of me. Of Past Ashley. And I want it back.

I also packed my cell phone and its charger. Maybe stupid—it's been dead for ages, and where am I supposed to find an electric outlet if I escape? But I'm a planner, and I may find a chance to use it somewhere. I may find a chance to call my mom. Tell her I'm sorry.

It feels weird leaving everything else behind after spending so much time and energy and money moving it all from California to Texas. All this furniture, that dead TV (which is basically just part of the furniture now), my coffee maker . . . but it's just stuff. Just dead skin I've gotta shed.

And that's it. I'm probably forgetting something. Like a weapon? Maybe I should pack a knife or two. I don't know, Diary. How the fuck do you pack for a trip whose destination is just a big fucking question mark?

. . .

Someone's knocking at the front door.

18

JACQUELINE & ASHLEY

"These men have no badges or identification of any kind, and they refuse to provide one when asked. They are showing up in unmarked vans and abducting protestors, and they seem to be acting on orders straight from the White House. As you can see behind me, these men are shooting grenades of some kind into the peaceful protestors' faces at point-blank range, and— [flinches at loud report] Guns have started going off! People are running and— No, stop, what are you doing? I'm a journalist— Help! No— [rustling mic sounds, feedback, sound is cut]"

—Portland, Oregon, reporter just moments before she was taken, on live television, by masked men in military dress and beaten in full view of the cameras; her and her crew's whereabouts are currently unknown

BOOM!
A gigantic thud, from somewhere close—

BOOM! BOOM!

The scattering of embers that floated around her like somnambulistic fireflies died into afterimages. The flower bud she cupped in her palm, open for her just moments before, now shriveled into itself and darted through her fingers, disappearing into its hidey-hole like a sea anemone.

BOOM! BOOM! BOOM!

"It's finally happening, Jackie boy."

She spun around, toward the bedroom door, her heart thudding so hard it might break through her brittle ribcage. But it was just the Cardigan Man, leaning against the inside of the closed door. He had dressed, sliding back into his faded jeans and *Helter Skelter* tee.

"What's happening?" she asked. Her voice barely hovered above a whisper.

He grinned. "You know."

"No, I don't, why would I . . . ?"

Her voice trailed off, darted back inside her throat like the flowers. Hiding. Because she *did* know . . . didn't she?

"Ash is leaving," she rasped.

His grin grew. "She's leaving *you*."

Jack's throat was as dry as parchment. Her body's glow, which had sung itself back to a healthy amber as her flowers sipped the open air, began to curdle and diminish again.

"About time, if you ask me," he said, his words like a punch to her gut. "Bitch was making you sick."

She swallowed, and found she could breathe easier.

"Yeah," she agreed.

* * *

Boom! BOOM! BOOM—
CRASH!

It was a colossal effort to control her breathing. Ash's entire body was desperate to inhale huge gasps of oxygen, to ready her for a flight—or fight—for her life. Her blood thudded in her ears. The world crowded around her in a massive *whomp* of adrenaline that made her vision spotty. Dust filled her lungs and stuck to her sweaty head under the couch. In the panicky, interminable seconds after those first booming knocks on the front door, she'd scribbled in her journal about it and then thought, *What if they're here to kill me? Finish the job because they couldn't lure me out like Mo. Shouldn't I hide instead of recording my final testament in this fucking diary?* She'd dropped pen and journal and body and scurried under the couch mere milliseconds before the front door crashed open.

In the silence that followed, the buzzing insect song of Texas in summer flooded inside, almost covering the crunch of boots as someone entered the apartment. Bright, life-giving sunlight bathed the entire apartment with color. She would never last hidden under this couch.

As if she'd bent the weather to her needs, however, clouds suddenly billowed across the sun, draping shadows over everything like the sediment of a disturbed ocean floor. Ash cowered into a tighter ball, her stomach clenched to control her shuddering breaths so her predator, that great white shark swimming into her apartment, wouldn't hear her and devour her.

Why didn't they come in the middle of the night? her mind blared. *Catch me in bed, like last time?*

"Mask up, boys," someone said.

Someone else scoffed. "I don't smell anything."

"The bodies didn't just evaporate, dumbass," the first someone said, his voice now muffled. "They're probably busy rotting in the bedroom. But hey, suck down that chink's bat disease if you want. Not my funeral."

Ash almost gasped at that word: *chink*. She *knew* that voice, didn't she? It had been so long since she'd last heard it—almost a year now, surely—but hate crimes weren't easily forgotten.

That chink's muff suffocating you?

Down by the river, across town. Their first day in a new city, Austin, the weird-and-proud-of-it liberal bubble of Texas. At a screening of Ash's all-time favorite movie, the 1975 first-ever-blockbuster cinematic masterpiece, Steven Spielberg's *Jaws*.

It was the Cardigan Man.

Suddenly Ash felt incredibly small. Just as she had when she'd first met that monster, with his superior sneer and the way he only spoke to Jack because *Ash*, the dirty yellow mongrel, was beneath him, beneath both of them. She was just a *thing* that belonged to her lesbo lover, a thing Jack kept around for a lark until she got bored and was ready for a real man like him.

She felt small, and she felt control of her own self being pulled from her grasp. An absurd image occurred to her in the dark: her, scurrying across the apartment floor, a tiny, scared little mouse; and him, with his big, stomping boots and wielding the broom like a weapon, chasing her and laughing and calling out "Heeeeeere, chinky leso bitch, heeeeeeere" and finally cornering her and consigning her to Mo's same fate, and then the Cardigan Man and fucking Doug enjoying Ashley-kabob over a campfire in the middle of the apartment floor.

That thought pinged something in the back of her memory, bringing her back to the present. The broom. It was still here—right there in fact, just barely in arm's reach. She snaked her hand out from under the couch, pinching the bristles and sliding the broom toward her from where it still lay flat on the floor by the wall.

Another voice she recognized, this one also muffled, made her stop cold.

"Bitches never paid last month's rent, you know that?"

Fucking Doug.

There was a pause, in which Ash was sure her former landlord expected commiserating "Oh wow, those cheap motherfuckers" and "You sure got the last word, then, huh?"

But the Cardigan Man said, "You imprisoned your tenants and left them to die, Doug. What did you expect?"

Another awkward pause, then Doug said, "I'm just saying."

Cardigan Man chuckled. "You're a fucking psycho, man."

More crunching footsteps. Ash couldn't see the entrance, since the couch faced the opposite direction, toward the sliding-door window, but from the sound, she guessed someone else was climbing into the apartment through the bashed-in front door.

Another voice she thought she recognized, though she couldn't be sure—one of the Cardigan Man's friends from the river? "The fag downstairs kept a pretty big safe in his closet. Might be worth hiring that guy who said he could crack 'em."

Doug laughed derisively. "Kept it in his closet. John

always had a queer sense of humor."

Ash clutched the broom tighter, wanting to scream. *John* . . .

Cardigan Man ignored Doug. "Just drag the safe to my truck and keep tossing each unit till you hit the end of the building. You don't have to come report every little thing to us. Jesus."

The new guy sounded put out. "I'm just saying—"

"And *I'm* just saying this place isn't exactly secluded. There's a fucking firehouse just up the road. What if one of these fuckers managed to survive this long and then go snag some firemen and they come over here with the cavalry and we're just diddling around taking inventory with our thumbs up our asses?"

Ash called bullshit on *that* happening. The men had brought a whole goddamn firing squad down on Mo, just a week after she'd lost track of the state of the world outside the apartment; that had been world-ending loud, yet not a single fucking fireman had come to investigate. She'd always assumed that if they did they were dead. What would they rescue her with, hoses?

But apparently the new guy wasn't smart enough— or maybe he wasn't *dumb* enough—to tell the Cardigan Man he was full of shit. The next thing Ash heard was his receding grumbles while his footsteps crunched back out the front entrance and along the walkway outside.

Quickly, not letting herself think about what she was doing, Ash used the noise of the new guy climbing out over a splintered and fallen front door to mask her own movements. She twisted the broom handle over and over until it came free from its bristle base. It would have been faster to untwist the base itself, but she didn't dare stick it out from under the couch so it could have full range of movement.

Now she had her weapon. Not ideal—there was really only so much damage one could do with a hollow stick of titanium. She felt a surge of anger at herself for being so foolish—why didn't she pack knives, too, or anything more useful? Her backpack stared at her across the carpet, peeking out around the antique chest that served as a coffee table. She'd left it propped up against the big window, since that was originally where she thought she'd stage her escape, just as Mo had. If she had packed knives, surely she could have crawled to it from here and grabbed a big bread knife before anyone spotted her.

Her heart thumped impossibly loud, like someone was tapping an amplified microphone before a speech; Ash expected one of the men to hear her heartbeat, find her, and call out for backup. Her last sight would be of those gathering storm clouds outside a big-ass window she'd never break through—

But no. Somehow, incredibly, both men trampled loudly down the hallway, not bothering to venture farther into the main room just yet. She held her breath, listening, wondering:

What will happen to Jack if they find her?

This was the one thought that might stop Ash from attempting to escape, and she knew it—yes, she was *leaving* Jack, but that didn't mean she wanted her to be *murdered*, she wasn't heartless—so she threw it from her head with desperate, frightened resolve, and crawled out from under the couch.

"What the fuck are you *doing*?"

Ash froze. For one heart-stopping moment, she

thought the Cardigan Man was talking to *her*, was about to come barreling out of the hallway and throttle her. She squeezed the broom handle so tight her hands screamed in pain.

"This is the bedroom, I thought I'd—"

"Yeah, I *know* it's the bedroom, I lived in this building, too, dumbass."

Ash breathed silently in relief and thought, *He's talking to Doug, not me.*

"But that's probably where the bodies of those two carpet-munchers are." The Cardigan Man's grim chuckle, behind his mask, reminded her ridiculously of Darth Vader. "Let's leave it for last."

"Oh," Doug said, his voice barely audible behind his mask. "Right."

"I'll make quick work of this closet, see what they got in here. You check out the bathroom. There's probably some good shit in the medicine cabinet. The hot one gave me serious psycho vibes. Like, certifiable."

The hot one. He thought of Jacqueline as the "hot one," the woman with the classic feminine bombshell looks, and Ashley would always just be the *chink.*

She finally unfroze and tiptoed past the hallway toward the broken front door. Doug had disappeared into the bathroom. The Cardigan Man had his upper torso shoved into the hallway closet, and he was busy rummaging around. She felt the sudden urge to take the sharp, screwed end of the broom handle and shove it up his ass, which peeked out past the accordioned closet door as if daring her to do it.

But she suppressed this feeling and crept to the entrance, smelling fresh, humid outside air for the first time in what felt like forever.

The front door resembled a splintered heap of kindling and driftwood. Strips and scraps of soldered metal framing curled and bent around it like the cored-out remains of Wolverine's skeleton. A big hunk of black steel lay to the side of it all, and she realized how they'd broken inside: it was one of those battering rams, like in a cop movie when a SWAT team descended on the bad guy and busted through a door that had fifty different locks and bolts keeping it shut.

She paused before this mess. She might be able to leap over it all and sail through the doorframe and out onto the walkway, but it would still make noise, and she had to be prepared to run. She was barefoot, but bloody feet were an easy price to pay for her freedom. She looked back, suddenly wishing she'd thought to dart to the window and grab her backpack, but now it was too late for that. The closet and bathroom were small. One or both of those men would come waltzing back into the main room any second now, and her chance at escape would plummet toward zero.

She turned back toward the front door and bent her knees, taking steady breaths—

And then she saw it.

And realized walking through that door would be the same as walking into the jaws of the beast. Out of the frying pan and into the fire.

Gunfire. Like the tornado of gunfire that had swept Mo away. That blaze of death still roared in Ash's memory, rooting her to the spot.

What she saw through the hole where her front door used to be were trucks. *Dozens* of trucks. Just over the lip of the walkway, in the gravel parking lot below, sat trucks like the ones she'd seen in all the apocalypse movies, the ones where the lines between government-funded military and guerilla militiamen were blurred beyond distinction. A few even had huge, monstrous gun turrets secured to their beds, casually pointing up into the sky but ready to turn toward her with their big bores and shoot death straight into her.

And she heard them, too. That chorus of insects had fled the thickening storm clouds, and in its place were the sounds of organized looting: boots, commands, forced entry, packing and driving, dozens of men surely on that very walkway just feet away and probably armed. What would she do, grab that fire extinguisher outside the door and bash her way to freedom? She wouldn't make it ten feet.

A voice startled her: "Fucking nothing in there, man, looks cleaned out."

Doug.

And the Cardigan Man: "Well, get started in the main room, then."

Footsteps, coming her way.

She was stuck.

THE CARDIGAN MAN'S SKIN was boiling away from his face.

"You lied to me," Jack said, still sitting on the bed.

"Oh, for fuck's sake." His glass-churning laughter coughed out of a jaw that gleamed bone-white. His beard was curling into black shrivels and falling from his face, griming his T-shirt with soot. "Jackie boy, I set you *free.*"

She scooted across the mattress, closer. "You *lied*. I can hear you—the *real* you—out there"—she jabbed a finger toward the door he still leaned against, at the rummaging sounds just through the hallway—"and you can, too. You know you're not really here. You're not the Cardigan Man, or whatever his fucking name is. You're fake, you're my paranoia, you're my fear, a hallucination—"

He barked a laugh. "Then whose cock have you been stuffing yourself with?"

"—you're not real and you're not *here* and neither is *Ash* and *you made me stab Ash*—"

She slapped a hand over her mouth. Tears streamed down her face.

Ash. Ashley. She was alone now, Ash had left her, left her because of this fucking monster, because of her fear—

Reading her thoughts, the Cardigan Man leaned forward, leering as more of his skin withered and shriveled tight against his waxy scalp and then rotted away in strands of jerky. "You're the monster here, Jackie boy. If you say I'm not here, that just leaves *you*."

Jack cried harder, could barely breathe from crying.

He was right. It was just her.

Just Jack. *She* was the monster.

She looked down at her body. She was still naked—completely naked now that the bandages were off her feet. She looked down at her bare body, seeing only that of a monster.

And she began to change.

19

ASHLEY & JACQUELINE

"President Calls for Delayed Election, Sends National Guard Marching Throughout Major Cities, Retreats to Bunker"

—*The New York Times*
July 2020

R.I.P. the United States of America, July 4 1776–July 4 2020

@DanRather
11:59 PM · July 4, 2020
2.5M RTs 13M likes

ASH WAS A DEER IN HEADLIGHTS.

She'd never understood that feeling, never understood how an animal whose entire existence turned on the axle of survival could just stand there, frozen, as impending death swept toward it. But now that was exactly what she'd become: starved, her eyes bugging from her sunken skull, just one bounding leap from freedom, yet locked within the tractor beam of an oncoming predator. Her, the deer; the headlights, converging on all sides.

The armored trucks and countless men just outside the door.

Doug, fucking Doug, a single step from spotting her, lunging at her, *killing* her—

"Hah . . . X marks the spot."

This from Doug, muffled and muttering to himself, as he strode from the hall—

—and right past her.

He'd entered the main room at an oblique angle, homed in on something beyond the couch, which bisected the exact center of the living space. Ash was, miraculously, beyond his peripherals. He would have had to look over his shoulder to catch her standing there, just feet from the front entrance, her bare foot brushing against the heavy battering ram.

She didn't breathe. Didn't move.

With just three long strides—Doug was a tall, lanky man, his face pockmarked and severe—he'd reached his destination: the antique chest. Ash supposed, in his dumb, greedy view of the world, he looked at their coffee table and thought, *Treasure! For me! X marks the spot!*

He fell to his knees as if to prostrate himself before the chest and pray to the pirate gods, and he fumbled momentarily with the locking mechanism. It was rusted and falling apart, really just achieving an aesthetic design rather than anything so utilitarian as security. He'd find the chest empty, with two or three throw blankets at the bottom from winter.

Finally, her legs unlocked. She could move. She entertained the thought of picking up the battering ram and bashing his brains in, but she knew without even trying that it would be far too heavy for her starved little body to wield on her own. The way he'd fallen to his knees gave her another idea, though: he was now at the perfect height for her to steal into the kitchen, retrieve one of those bread knives she'd forgotten to pack, and stab its serrated tip down along his spinal column.

But the moment the thought flitted into her brain she knew she wouldn't be able to go through with it. She couldn't stoop to this man's level, couldn't join him in the murderers' club. Because that's all he was now: a murderer, returning to the scene of the crime to loot the bodies, a modern-day Thenardier seizing opportunity in 2020 America, and this apartment building was his Parisian sewers.

"Hey, boss, we got somethin' for ya!"

Someone was jogging down the walkway, a mere second from popping through the front door, and Doug was already awkwardly turning on his knees to face the voice—and Ash.

She darted to the hallway.

She could have ducked into the kitchen, but that was a dead end, would only be buying a few seconds, and then she'd *have* to grab a knife to defend herself. The hallway was her only answer.

She almost ran smack dab into the Cardigan Man.

Holding her breath, not daring to breathe, she stopped just inside the hall. He was still shoved into the closet, shifting things around and swearing and grunting, his ass, in a pair of faded Levi's, hunched out into the hallway. The closet door, a thin wood number that squeaked out on tracks and folded like an accordion, opened toward the main room and front entrance and thankfully blocked his peripheral vision both times she had darted past.

She edged around him, pressing herself against the wall.

On his other side, he'd stacked a few boxes he'd pulled from the closet, and the bathroom door, which Doug must have left open as he went to go find his buried treasure, was using those boxes as a doorstop.

"This *shitting* thing won't *open*," Doug grunted from the main room.

Of the two options available to her—the bedroom or the bathroom—the bedroom door was the only one completely out of the Cardigan Man's sight. But it was closed, and Ash didn't trust her ability to secret it open without an audible *click* or the hinges squeaking or the spring in the cheap doorknob creaking. Plus, there was no way he'd miss the horrifying stench that would pounce into the hall the second that door snicked open, even through that N95 mask he wore.

"*What* 'shitting thing'?" the Cardigan Man called, his head still shoved in the closet. "You find something good?"

That left the open bathroom door. Before she could lose her nerve, she squeezed the broom handle still in her grasp, careful not to let it bang into anything around her, and practically slid into the bathroom.

Doug called, "You got something—"

"Figure it out yourself," the Cardigan Man growled. "I'm busy!"

She made it. She grinned in giddy relief.

Then, the grin vanishing, she thought:

Now what?

THE FLOWERS HAD COME back out to play.

Jack sang to them, humming softly:

"Dun dunnn . . . dun dunnn . . . dun-dun-dunnn . . ."

Their buds split open and welcomed her. Their embers sifted through the air, pulsating to the rhythm of her melody, dancing before her. Her legs, pulled up onto the mattress and turned in a loose, semi-Indian-style position, continued to fruit and split and bloom and yield a harvest of flowers. First, along her ankle and up her Achilles heel, and then up from there along the delicate swell of her calf. She noted with calm serenity how the meat of her calf seemed to deflate, and this made a kind of symmetrical sense to her: the flowers were her, the *embers* were her, just like the glow was hers, and so they had grown from parts of her body. She was transforming into something new, perhaps, but it was still her, still the essential parts.

The flowers continued up the insides of her legs, now tickling the bottoms of her thighs, and she laughed. It was as if she were wearing thigh-high leather boots, and these two split seams of skin were the tied laces and zippers.

A fleeting thought: *Morgan Kiner can't see* this *on Google Images.*

And then: *Morgan who . . . ?*

"What the fuck is happening to you?"

She looked up, almost surprised there was someone else. The Cardigan Man. He was still there, except now he was wearing his cardigan—again, in summer, how ridiculous—and his beard was burned from his face and the last remnants of skin clung to his blackened skull. His gasmask sat atop his head, like a crown—she supposed that was the only way he could wear it now, without ears to hold the leather straps. He grinned at her, marsh lights burning in the black holes of his eyes, but the grin was terrified, a dog when it stumbles across a wolf.

"I mean, what the fuck, right, Jackie boy? What is this shit, like, some miracle of evolution or abomination or . . . ?"

She didn't respond. She just looked at him, and his grin grew more strained.

"Your hair's gone," he said. "All fallen out, like a cancer patient."

But she didn't care what he said.

She didn't care what *anyone* said. Not anymore.

She looked straight into his fiery, eldritch eye sockets, and told him:

"Leave."

And he did.

ASH'S ADRENALINE was an ocean's roar in her eardrums.

She had no idea what the new arrival was telling Doug, but she was fairly certain it had nothing to do with her. Even if, for some reason, Doug had snipers or lookouts on the other side of the building, peeping through all the big sliding-door windows, she didn't think she could have been spotted. The sunlight had been bright enough that she didn't have to sit with her back against the window and she had been journaling while lying on the couch. After the *BOOM! BOOM! BOOM!* of the battering ram, she'd dropped behind the antique chest and been completely out of sight.

So she didn't care. Maybe they'd found a gold mine in one of the other apartments, or the coven of witches had booby-trapped their apartment with a few nasty surprises for intruders.

The only thing she cared about was that question: *Now what?*

No opening. No options. No windows led out to the walkway from the bathroom: it was all one solid wall with a mirror and medicine cabinet and then tile where the shower started.

But Doug had already searched the bathroom. Maybe, if she managed to close the door without being noticed, she could hole up in here until they were gone. Maybe she didn't have to find a way out yet.

She edged back to the open door, peeking out. She could see the cardboard and plastic sides of the assorted boxes stacked just behind it. No way could she close the door and be lucky enough that the Cardigan Man would just think, what, that's a self-closing door with a delay? A gust of wind? No, he'd be immediately suspicious and investigate, and then Ash would have to find out how tough this broom handle really was.

The bathroom was small enough that anyone moving down the hallway to the bedroom door would have a clear view of every nook and cranny in here.

An idea, almost eliciting a gasp: Could she lay flat in the tub?

She rushed to the shower, raising one leg to climb in—

She stopped, almost having to wheel her arms comically so she didn't teeter over.

The tub was still full of water.

Goddammit.

She couldn't risk the sloshing or even the most minuscule displacement of water. The bathroom acoustics would echo right out into the Cardigan Man's ears and he'd come in here and drown her in her own bathtub.

That left the walk-in closet.

The pocket door might make the slightest noise as it rolled on its tracks, but it really was the best option. She could either make more noise trying to hide or wait for someone to spot her out in the open . . . or she could retreat into Jack's old cocoon of clothes and think of something else.

She slid the door open halfway, as slowly and silently as she could, and slipped into the opening, pressing the door closed behind her.

Her heart only came down from her throat and stopped its timpani beat in her ears after a full minute pressed behind the hanging wall of clothing, waiting and waiting for someone to follow her in here because they heard something, waiting and waiting until she was sure there would be nothing.

For the moment, she amended.

It didn't reek in here like it had the last time she'd been inside. And at that thought, memories of that confrontation rushed at her like those headlights splattering her deer brains all over the tarmac: Jack, smelling like week-old tripe . . . Jack, grabbing at Ash's crotch and telling her to *show me that cock* . . . Jack, her voice as dead as that smell, saying, "I'll kill you," and plunging a knife into Ash's hand—

The knife!

Ash sat up. Of course—the smell was gone because

Jack hadn't been in here since that day either. Which meant the steak knife was most likely still in here, as well as—

Ash's hands fell on a plastic cylinder, and she clutched at it, searching for a button. She clicked it and a scythe of white light cut through the folds of clothing. She whipped it frantically around the carpeted space. It hadn't even occurred to her that she could have stepped on a knife and cut her foot when she came in here, probably crying out with the surprised pain and alerting the men to her presence.

A single stiletto heel, discarded—no.

The plate and chicken bones, covered in squirming ants—no.

There, stuck to the carpet fibers with black dried blood: the knife.

Just as she picked it up, the pocket door leading to the bathroom slid open.

JACK'S ROOM WAS AGLOW with a pulsating lightshow of embers, and she was dancing to its rhythm. After the flowers had split the seams of her inner thighs, she'd had to stand for fear of crushing them. They opened up and moved in the air like an army of linked antennae calibrating one another's frequency. The petals linked with the embers, casting her aura across the bedroom like a fisherman's net about to reel in the day's catch. And with them, with such a vast and complete network of herself, she saw . . . *everything*. And she danced in such pregnant knowledge. She danced on the mattress. After so long being unable to put her weight on her heels, her muscles had reconfigured and reshaped themselves and she held herself like a minotaur; she stood a few inches higher than she used to, as if she were wearing Ashley's stilettos for some big night out. And her mind whispered: *Ashley who . . . ?* but it knew who Ashley was, it still knew the pain of what she'd done to her wife—she'd *stabbed* her, she'd pierced her with a knife until the D word had hissed out like escaping helium, DIVORCE!, or perhaps it had left Ash like escaping *hydrogen* and had combusted with the oxygen needed in order to say the D word and then one of Jack's aura embers had sparked it and now Ash was the Hindenburg, a big ball of shimmering flame floating down to the earth and never to embark on its maiden voyage. Now Jack stood on the mattress on the balls of her feet and she danced. The Cardigan Man was no more. She'd eaten him. It had *appeared* as if he'd just simply blinked out of existence, but Jack knew better. Jack knew now that he had never been the *real* Cardigan Man. Indeed, maybe there had never actually ever *been* a Cardigan Man—after all, who wears cardigans in hundred-degree humidity? That creature with the grinning skull and glorious cock had never been real, just like Jack had never been a real wife, had just been playacting on a lark like fucking Daisy Buchanan with her plaything, Tom. The Cardigan Man was really just a mirror image of *her*, of Jackie boy, and maybe even a real, tangible part of her, not just a mirage. That thought had shown her how empty she was without him, and so she'd eaten him. She'd sucked him down like a vampire sucking blood, slurped his hipster beard and toned muscles and gasmask and guttural laughter and grinning skull and marsh-fire eyes and decayed skin and cardigan and cartilage and testosterone and they'd all flown helter-skelter across the bedroom, straight to her gullet. The millions of floating embers had scattered to make room for the Cardigan Man's essence, and he'd zoomed down her throat and he'd left fertile pollen on the petals of her flowers and she'd glowed brighter than ever before. She'd filled herself with him, and moaned with pleasure, the pleasure of seeing oneself plainly and peeling away the skin to get to the grinning skull and saying, *I see you, I know you, I am you*, and reveling in the fear. The Fear. It swirled in her gut like lavender milk. Yes, the Cardigan Man, that watchful demon, was gone, but he would never truly be gone, not while he sloshed around in her tummy, tickling that stretch of skin between her belly button and her pubic hair and sending not butterflies swirling but moths, thick luna moths with moondust sifting from their wings. She'd sucked him down like helium, so she could speak her *own* words, whatever she wanted without fear of the consequences, because *Jesus* wasn't watching, nor Mom or Dad or Ash, because they were all dead now—or maybe she'd sucked him down like hydrogen, and now *she* was the airship on its maiden voyage, just seconds away from combustion and a beautiful, fireball death. She didn't fear death. It didn't do to fear what lurks in your heart.

"*Dun dun . . . dun dunnn,*" she sang, dancing.

The Fear *was* death.

20

ASH

"President Trump Makes Satire Impossible; Go
Fuck Yourself, America"
—*The Onion*, July 2020
last headline before the satire website went dark

JACK'S COCOON of hanging clothes felt like Ash's grave.

The fabric, nylons and scratchy wools and heavy
coats and wrinkled cotton, pressed in around her as the
pocket door slid a slow, silky *phffffffffft*. She fumbled with
the flashlight, killing its bulb, but her heart, slamming in
her chest, shouted *itstoolateitstoolateitstoolate*—

The curtain of clothes screamed along the metal ring
as someone ripped them violently away from her. The
flashlight wrenched away, clipping her on the chin as it
was grabbed from her, and again she was a deer in the
headlights and the headlight that would freeze her in
place was that flashlight and the car that would run her
over would be—

"Who do we have here?"

Click.

She managed enough movement to flinch away from

the expected blinding beam, but it wasn't aimed at her. It shone straight up, illuminating the intruder's face like he was about to tell a scary story around a campfire and send all the little campers screaming into the woods. The light was harsh; it brought out sharp angles in his face like a jack-o'-lantern, his wicked grin carved across the gourd of his face with a knife—

The knife!

For the second time, Ash remembered that steak knife, clutched in her hand, caked with dried chicken grease and her own old blood but surely still sharp.

The Cardigan Man leered down at her, his face a writhing mask of shadow puppets.

"Well, well, if it isn't the cunt's whore—"

"HAAH!"

A formless scream yanked itself from her gut as she swung her clenched fist at him, unconsciously mirroring her own wife, in this same closet, stabbing out at who she thought was this same man—this "Cardigan Man," the ghost that had haunted their marriage for the last eleven months now.

The knife connected and stuck. He grunted.

Inexplicably, a river smell struck Ash at the same moment she struck the Cardigan Man, almost as if she'd let it out of him with the knife, and she was washed away to that first harbinger of the end last August. This man, intruding on two strangers' lives and spitting vile hatred at them—but not hatred . . . fear. He had been afraid of them, really.

And he would be afraid of her now.

She gripped the knife's handle and twisted, cutting a scream from his throat, letting it out like escaping air, like that escaping river smell. He screamed again.

"You fucking *bitch*!"

"No," she said, her heart beating so hard it caused her voice to jump up and down. "No, *you're* the bitch!"

Not her best comeback, but she didn't care—she was aware now of the flashlight once more, its wandering light stabbing her vision, and before he could wield it as a blunt weapon she pitched forward, tackling him.

His *"Oof!"* of surprise was like music to her ears—he hadn't expected a fight from such a tiny, insignificant thing as her, but he had been wrong.

Now she was on top of him, straddling his body, the knife still stuck in his shoulder and tight in her grip. In a flash, she saw an immediate future where she unsheathed the knife from his body and plunged it down again and again, putting all her weight on the blade until it hacked its way to his still-beating heart and she let the river smell out of that thumping organ and his screams ran out of air and he died with his grin flipped upside down—

But again, no. Just like with Doug, she knew she couldn't. She wouldn't. This wasn't her, and she refused to be anything other than *her*, than *Ashley*, ever again. Not for this man or the other men out there or for Jacqueline or whatever it was Jack had become, not for her mom or dad or uncle or Trump's America or anyone but Ash, *Ashley*. Her. She was under no one's control but herself.

"Fuck off me!" the Cardigan Man screamed.

He bucked beneath her and threw her bodily from him—sure, she was fit and strong, but also barely half his body weight—and she plunged into the darkness and came crashing against the door.

The bedroom door.

Jack . . .

She scrambled to her feet.

And stepped away from the door, from the bedroom.

From Jack.

From her past.

Vaulted over the man still struggling on the carpet.

And toward her future.

"COCAINE, A WHOLE DUFFEL of the stuff, just sitting in two K, man—"

The words barely registered as Ash burst from the bathroom, danced around the stuff pulled from the closet, and entered the main living space.

Two men stood like statues, staring at her, mouths gaping like fish.

"What the *fuck*?"

This from the one on the right, closest to Ash. It was Doug, his N95 mask pulled down and tucked under his chin. He stared at her, shocked, as if Elvis had just strolled out here to tell him the toilet was clogged. Behind him, she noticed, the TV was missing; they must have taken it already, and for some reason this felt absurd, because who watched television anymore during the apocalypse?

The other man, a weaselly little guy with a scraggly pube-beard, stood just past the twisted remains of the front door. The duffel bag he was carrying fell to his feet as he stared.

"Is she real, man?" the new guy whispered. His eyes were bugging out of his face. Ash noticed a dusting of white powder in the pubes of his mustache. "She here to take us to Hell?"

This was just absurd enough to slap Doug back into action. He took his eyes from Ash and shot the other guy a glare. "Andrew, you fucking dumbass, it's coke, not PCP. Go get backup!"

The weaselly man—coked-up Andrew—turned to leave, seemed to reconsider, turned back to them, and grabbed the duffel bag from the floor.

"Don't bother with the drugs, you moron!" Doug screamed.

Andrew stumbled, almost leaving emptyhanded, but still hugged the duffel to his chest before leaping over the busted door, tripping on the metal frame scraps, and face-planting out in the hallway.

Ash saw her chance. She could jump after him, easily side-step him.

But could she side-step *all* of them? All the men out there doing Doug's bidding?

"Look, I hate for it to have happened like this—"

She turned from the door. Doug. Doug was talking to her . . . *reasonably.* As if all this was a misunderstanding.

"—but, uh, obviously you and your roommate won't be getting back your deposit. I mean, *look* at this place, who's gonna pay for—"

She couldn't believe what he was saying. Had she gone in shock? Was she still in the closet with the Cardigan Man, his hands around her neck and her face a bloated shade of blue?

No. This was real.

Fucking DOUG.

A scream of inarticulate rage burst from her for the second time that day, and she rushed at him. The last thing she saw before bulldozing her shoulder into his ribs was his expression of complete surprise, as if there was no way a woman—be it Ash or any other—would ever think to tackle a man like Doug.

They tumbled over the couch together, Doug falling backward and managing to grab Ash's tank top hanging loosely over her bony shoulders and pull her down with him. They flew over the couch's back and landed on the cushions, her on top of him. Ash experienced a brief flash of memory: all the times she and Jack had done the same thing, giggling, kissing. The memory revolted her now—that life was over, and this was a man who had bullied her and attempted to starve her to death.

His hands were all over her head, like tarantulas, fighting for purchase, but there was no hair long enough to grab. Before he could try grabbing anywhere else or gouge her eyes out, she continued her momentum, rolling her body off the other side of the couch. She had her hands grabbed tightly onto his body—even her left hand, still swaddled in gauze from Jack's stabbing—and *yanked* with all her might.

He rolled off the couch with her, their positions switched so that Ash was the one on the bottom. She yanked again, and managed to work the inertia into a blunt weapon, sending Doug flying over her and crashing into the antique chest. There was an audible *thunk!* as Doug's temple connected with the chest's metal-studded corner.

Dead weight collapsed onto her. Now Ash was on the carpet between the couch and the chest, with Doug's revolting body slackly draped over her. She tried not to breathe in, pushing him so that she could slither out from beneath. It was so much more difficult than she'd expected—Doug was tall, sure, but he was also skinny, a pockmarked scarecrow, his limbs seemingly everywhere. Her body was weak, telling her it was done, it was tired, it needed to lay still until she fed it some protein, maybe another one of those delicious mice, please?

She used the antique chest to pull herself up, finally free, and took a few moments to breathe. Her chest heaved. Spots danced in her vision. Her hand wound ached.

And still she was so far away from escaping this place.

That Andrew guy would be here any minute with backup—backup that would probably be toting a few assault rifles and come in guns blazing.

She looked around frantically for things she could use against the window. Why hadn't she thought this through before? All her packing and planning, and she was just going to *die* here because she couldn't shatter a single pane of glass?

Her bare foot hit something metal; it clinked against the chest.

She looked down. "Well, fuck me," she said, and almost laughed.

A crowbar lay against one side of the antique chest.

And then she did laugh. Doug must have retrieved it to get into his precious "treasure chest." She was surprised he didn't throw it through the window himself when he finally got inside to find nothing but some shitty blankets.

But she couldn't lose time. She scooped it up, getting a feel for its weight in both hands, then rushed to the window and swung the crowbar like a baseball bat.

The claw at the curved end of the crowbar kissed the glass then punched through as easily as if through paper.

Cracks spiderwebbed out from the epicenter in the blink of an eye, and Mo's words echoed across to her from his grave:

Cheap glass just needs an excuse to fall apart.

And he was right: it was almost shocking how fast the outside world was hidden behind a scrim of thousands of interconnected cracks.

But before she could give the glass that final reason to fall out of its frame, a sudden cascade of water hit her from behind—

And something hard slammed into the back of her head.

CLANG!

She crumpled to the ground.

A metal pot gonged against the carpet as it fell from her attacker's hands—one of the dozen or so big pots she'd filled and left around the apartment. Then those hands closed over her smarting head, and she couldn't make her fingers tighten around the crowbar to fight back.

Her body was failing. She'd die here, just inches from escape.

Those hands, like gnarled tree branches, yanked her back, pulled her bodily from the floor, twisted her around, and now she was staring up into the livid face of her landlord. Blood had seeped down from his temple and washed his entire face with red. He looked like the Devil.

"I knew you were trouble the moment you and that lady-friend of yours moved in, you little bitch." Still-dripping blood bubbled and frothed with his spit, churning around his mouth as he spoke. "All y'all are nothin' but a bunch of ungrateful cocksuckers! Do you know how *hard* it is to manage an entire building of you motherfuckers?! *I* gotta make a living, too! You ever think of *that?*" Still holding her by the back of the head, he reached down with his other hand to retrieve the crowbar from the floor. "What, it's suddenly my problem y'all can't keep a job? I'm supposed to suffer just 'cause you can't pay rent like a goddamn adult?"

A glint came into his eyes, shining white through his mask of blood.

He tossed away the crowbar, which clattered against the antique chest.

"You ain't gonna act like responsible adults, best thing to do's to treat you like a child."

She felt something against her suddenly, poking against rough denim, and her mind screamed at her, horrified—

"Give ya a spankin'."

He's got an erection!

This thought was almost enough to send her right back into deer-in-headlights mode, but she couldn't, she *wouldn't* let this man lord over her anymore, and so she reached with her right hand for that hard something pressing against her thigh. She grabbed, and he let out a surprised moan, and he shuddered, and she *twisted* and *yanked*—

He crumpled as easily as she had after he'd hit her with the kitchen pot. They fell together. For the second time, she found herself on the floor with this repulsive man on top of her.

Doug recovered much quicker than she'd expected. Before she could even consider her next move, his eyes were bulging out of their sockets again, his face a quivering rictus of rage.

"You *bitch*, I'll—"

His hands found her throat, and in mere seconds her vision was popping with a sky of falling stars, and she knew then that she was going to die.

No . . .

She raised her hands, flailing them futilely at his face, at his throat, at his hands wrapped around her neck, cords of muscle snaking up his arms as if etched in stone. She flapped them up her own, gasping face and above her head, and distantly she felt them crash through something.

Crumbling glass.

She'd fallen with her head mere inches from that great big sliding-door window, now zigzagged with a million cracks and waiting for that final push.

She gave it the excuse it needed, and it fell.

Somewhere behind the fizzing flares obscuring her vision she could see the glass raining down around her and Doug. She thought she saw him flinch back, but still his hands didn't loosen their viselike grip grinding her windpipe flat.

Shards of glass littered around them like diamonds, and humid outside air *whooshed* in through the newly gaping hole in the apartment, but still she wondered if she'd ever live to see another Texas summer storm.

Her left hand closed around something—not the crowbar, not the kitchen pot, not Doug's erect penis, but something hard and cutting. She clutched at it and raised it and the last thing she saw before her vision popped and fizzled to nothing was something glinting in her hand.

A shard of glass, big enough to grip—

And bring stabbing into Doug's bobbing throat.

Ash couldn't see what she was doing, but she felt it, and she heard it: a *glug* more than a scream, and a fountain of warm blood raining down on her, and still she sawed the glass shard back and forth across his neck, working blindly, barely feeling the glass against the thick gauze wrapped around her hand.

Somewhere in the mess, her airways peeked back open and she gasped in shuddering mouthfuls of air and blood and she was coughing on her side now, coughing up blood, *Doug's* blood, and somewhere along the way he'd died and fallen, this time to the side of her instead of atop her. More gracious in death than ever in life.

She gulped the humid air. Wiped her hands and then her face against her tank top, most of which was also drenched in blood. She felt like Carrie on that prom stage, and now she was convinced there was no *way* that crazy bitch would be able to see all those laughing teenagers with pig's blood in her eyes.

Between her hacking coughs, she heard something.

Footsteps. Running footsteps.

Fuck.

She wasn't free of this mess just yet.

Ash scrambled up, scattering bits of glass around her. She still struggled to breathe; she still saw spots. She kicked Doug's body, not caring if it hurt her foot, and screamed at him, but it came out weak and hoarse.

"Doug, you in there?!"

"Fuck," she said, turning from him—from the man who had made her a murderer—and grabbing the backpack, which had blessedly not fallen through the open window in the commotion. In her weakened state, she cursed whatever sentimental bullshit had made her pack all her journals and books. Stephen King's *The Stand* could literally be the death of her.

She inspected the window. Most of the glass had fallen completely away, with a few shards sticking haphazardly along the frame. Some of that glass lay like stardust on the carpet. She noticed a bloody footprint in their midst and realized she must have stepped on a shard and cut her bare foot. No time for shoes, though.

Through the window, the tree stood a solid ten feet away, with a strip of sidewalk one story below between the building and a steep incline to the water. She'd need a running start to reach the tree trunk, and even then she'd probably break something somewhere along the rough landing.

A scream and a shattering sound from the bathroom. Ash hesitated.

Jack...

She'd left her in there, with that monster, with the Cardigan Man. She turned to the hallway. She could hear someone emerging, and could it be—

Ash turned away, back toward the window, toward her escape. She was done with that, she was done with this life, and anyway, the thought of what might emerge from that hallway suddenly made her gorge rise in her throat, and she was afraid, so impossibly afraid, at what she might see. At what Jacqueline had become. She'd be crawling, Ash knew, just *knew*, crawling and covered in bedsores and scurvy, a grinning mouth of blood the only color among her bleached, sallow skin like parchment. She'd look like an utter nightmare. Like a concentration camp victim, clawing itself desperately from its living Hell. Ash felt a sharp stab of fear but swallowed it down.

I'm not afraid anymore, she thought. And it was true.

"The *fuck* did you do to Doug, you *bitch?*"

Men swarmed the front entrance, guns lifted.

Andrew and his backup, arrived to end the party.

So much for a running start, she thought.

And she jumped.

THE EXPECTED BULLETS, cutting her down from behind, never came.

That yawning gap between window and tree seemed to stretch impossibly before her as she flew through the thick air, reality unhinging its jaw to swallow her whole. Time clogged space. Any second now Ash expected to feel the teeth of biting bullets as the men came into the apartment and saw what she had done to their newly deceased leader. She expected death to rain down on her just as it had rained down on Mo, and then she expected real rain to come pouring down from the sky and wash away the blood.

BOOM!

She squeezed her eyes shut against the thunder of gunfire—

But it was *actual* thunder. No gunfire. No guns. No death flying to meet her.

She realized her mistake and opened her eyes a moment before impact.

The trunk of the tree rushed up to meet her. Time sped up; reality stitched its jaw back together. Her body slammed into the bark of the trunk. She crumpled around it like a ragdoll. A *crack!* nearly as loud as the thunder, or at least she thought so, until it was drowned out in another—

BOOM!

—and she was falling, her hands reaching too late to clutch at the vines that quilted the tree. The ground met her next. Another *crack!* like bone-dry kindling, and she realized it was in fact a bone, her right leg, broken somewhere below the knee.

But before she could even think about trying to stand up, gravity gave her a push, and her tumble continued. Down the slope of hill leading to the rocks and water below. Her senses were nothing but shades of green colliding with shades of pain. Vines and undergrowth made for poor cushioning and her body felt like a sack of ball bearings—or, perhaps more appropriately, a skin sack full of blood and bones and any second now those brittle calcium-deprived bones were going to puncture something vital and it would be *Game Over*. But this was no game—reality had rushed back toward her like a slingshot—and she wouldn't be respawning at the beginning of this Player 1 level. Dead was dead.

Gunmetal sky and green scrub revolved around her like a wheel she was the center of, over and over and flip and flop, until her body finally came to a juddering stop. She'd become too entangled in creepers to fall farther, and that was a small blessing—when the world finally stopped spinning, she saw that she'd come within feet of the sharp rocks that lined this shallow part of the creek.

BOOM!

And she thought, *Finally, FINALLY the bullets are coming, this pain can stop, everything can stop and I can rest—*

BOOM!

But again, it was thunder, not gunfire. And with it came the rain.

Texas rain, she'd discovered the previous summer, was a much heavier thing than what she'd experienced growing up in California. On the west coast, rain was light and cold and somehow freeing, and she used to like to run and dance beneath it and sing lines from *Singin' in the Rain*. Here, it was oppressive. It was nothing you wanted to get caught under. It covered the land like a lead blanket and then hammered itself into place until the world couldn't hold such a vast and growing amount of water. It came hot and heavy. It came fast and left whenever it pleased.

Now, the rain dug its fingers into every wound she'd accrued on her flying leap and subsequent fall from the apartment window. It made her cry out.

But it also made her keep going.

She pushed herself up from the undergrowth, put weight on her right leg—

And dropped like a stone, screaming.

She tried again, clenching her teeth yet still screaming through them, vibrating her jaw with her vented pain. Spots returned to her vision, but she managed to stand. In too much pain to look around, she hunched her shoulders and limped and hobbled like a zombie in a George Romero movie. She retained just enough awareness of her surroundings to put the creek to her left and follow its bank downstream.

She managed this way for perhaps a hundred feet, the rain pouring down and soaking her through and washing away all of Doug's blood and each new freshet of Ash's blood as it seeped from her countless wounds. The back-pack—which had managed to stay on her shoulders through the fall—would have the first-aid kit, but she didn't dare stop and try to bandage herself until she was somewhere safe. Besides, she knew that if she stopped now, she'd never get going again.

She came to the part of the creek where the cracked sidewalk angled haphazardly down the hill from the apartments. Finally she lifted her head and forced herself to take in her surroundings.

The trees soared above her, and the sidewalk and hill opened to a wide expanse of grass. A memory came to her: a younger, more naïve Ashley, stepping down here to check for signs of the Cardigan Man. She remembered thinking of this place as a cathedral. Now . . . now it felt like so much more. Now it was the jumping-off point for her new life. If it was a cathedral, then the double oak doors were thrown wide and God was commanding her to step through them and begin her pilgrimage.

She clung to the straps of her backpack, preparing herself for the precipitous climb up the grassy hill, and trekked to the canoes. She would be useless on her feet after too long, even if there *were* firemen at the nearby station ready to help her; she also held no doubt that any cars on the other side of the building would be completely blocked off from her by all those guerilla men with their turreted trucks.

That left the river.

Mo's original plan.

But she knew as soon as she reached the stack of canoes and kayaks that it would be impossible. Not in her state. She had no idea just how many bones she'd managed to break in her flight from the apartment window, but she counted at least two ribs and her leg—perhaps in multiple places. That coupled with internal bleeding and she'd die before she could muscle one of these halfway to the water.

Rain poured; thunder clapped.

Could she swim? Or maybe float? She'd have to leave her backpack behind . . .

She laughed, briefly entertaining the idea of using that stupid wedding-ring float still wasting away, corpselike, in the pool. The laugh threatened to turn into a sob.

She turned and stumbled back down the incline, re-tracing her steps all those months ago until she came to the little dock on the water. This was where tenants used to set off on their little adventures down the creek. She had watched them from her apartment window and thought, *That could be me!*

Well, it would be her now.

She stepped down the wooden stairs and around the little patio—

And again she laughed.

The dock had come fully into view. There, on a raft no bigger than a door laid flat, sat a canoe. A big one, too, and ready for use. It was navy blue, shiny and well-maintained, and something about it tickled the back of Ash's brain.

I'm hoping my canoe is where I left it. If so, I will be taking my canoe down the river.

"Mo," she said aloud, and laughed again. It was a pained, sad laugh.

He must have known, even before Doug did what he did, that a quick escape might be prudent. He must have set his canoe down here, damn what the neighbors might say, in case he needed it in a rush.

"Thank you, Mo." He'd helped her escape after all.

Helming such a big craft—it seemed far bigger than all the other canoes up on the grass—felt impossibly out of reach. She was tired to the point of wanting death. But, she reminded herself, if *Jaws*'s Brody and Hooper could swim out of the ocean after blowing up a great white, she could navigate her way to the river.

The last step down to the dock proper folded her legs under her, and she fell. She managed to angle her body, and she let it and the side of her heavy backpack slam against the side of the canoe. The boat slid and flipped into the water, and she slid and flipped herself, like she had with Doug over and off the couch, but far less graceful and far more painful.

After a few unsteady moments where she was sure the canoe would flip and she'd drown, pulled to the shallow rock bottom of the river by her books and journals, it steadied itself. She was floating now. She shrugged off the backpack, crying out as it brushed against countless wounds, and let it fall to the canoe's bottom. She found a lightweight oar—similar to that titanium broom handle, a strangely comforting weight in her hands—clipped under the lip of the canoe, and she began to row.

She considered her options briefly: ahead of her, somewhere, was the river, presumably. But thoughts of the firehouse made her hesitate. That lay behind her, somewhere up the road, and she had a vague idea that maybe the creek followed the road.

Then she remembered how she'd watched countless adventurers from that goddamn sliding-door window float off in that direction, and they always seemed to reappear almost immediately after. It was a dead end. And besides, the firehouse was probably deserted.

No, she wouldn't turn back. Only forward from here on out.

The rain let up after quickly filling the bottom six inches of her craft. The sky lifted. The thunder went to sleep. The humidity sung with peeping insects. Her skin felt fresh. Felt new. She was sailing Theseus's ship now, and just like Robert Shaw had said in *Jaws*, it was *her* ship. She was mate, master, pilot, and she was captain.

She laughed—

Then gunfire exploded behind her.

She tensed. Listened.

It wasn't close enough to be for her. Just a few quick bursts, somewhere among the apartments. She wondered if they had come from *her* apartment, if they were meant for her old roommate.

Jack . . .

But she stopped herself from turning around.

She looked forward, down the meandering creek, its waters bloated with the rain, and saw the sky peeking through the trees. That way lay the river.

That way lay her new life.

And nothing but hers.

The storm settled, the water was clear again, and in it she saw shoals of small fish. In the freshening air, she caught glimpses of sparks along the shore. As she floated along the water, they sparked again, and suddenly she knew what they were.

"Fireflies," she said.

She smiled, and finally she cried.

No, she did not know what lay ahead.

But, she knew, that was okay.

She wasn't afraid anymore.

21

THE FEAR

"The oldest and strongest emotion of mankind is fear . . ."

—H.P. Lovecraft
Supernatural Horror in Literature

THE FEAR STOOD NAKED in its lair. It slurped the air and tasted . . .

. . . him.

In a flash it was off the mattress, ripping the closet door from its hinges as easily as wings from a butterfly. It reveled in its new strength. It shuffled inside on its foreclaws, pushing through the constricting tunnel of fabrics, and found him on all fours, waiting for her.

Waiting for *her* . . . memories of a past life, from its *pupa* stage, when this man came across her in a similar prostrate position and . . .

Did they copulate?

Should The Fear make him its mate now?

No, its body sang, *no . . . you belong to no one.*

And then: *We're hungry . . . huuuuuunnnnngrryyyyyy . . .*

He turned at the sound of it entering the walk-in

closet and slowly climbed to his feet. Yanked something from his chest—a weapon, glinting, reflecting the light of The Fear.

"Come on, you cunt," he growled. *"Come on!"*

The Fear, laughing, lunged forward. His challenge turned to panic gurgling in his throat. Even before it descended upon him, pulling him back down to the carpet, it felt its flowers opening up wide to him, sipping the air and wanting to taste him, taste his drink.

"What, can't even take me to dinner first, just want to f—*ffuUAARGH!*"

Its body opened, an armored flower of scales and teeth, the teeth chaotic rows of needling jags like those of a shark, a great white, the teeth zippering down its limbs and spine and opening wide for their meal.

It fed. Flowered petals and glinting teeth suckered themselves to his skin like barnacles to a ship's prow.

He screamed.

The Fear drank in that, too.

Viscous strings of black blood whipped themselves upon the throats of the flowers. They sang contentedly. The Fear roared. It brought its jaws, wide, down upon him. Clothing and skin pulled clean from the body. Still he screamed, louder, wordlessly. Words would have meant nothing, but The Fear understood the screams perfectly.

Its meal shucked to the meat beneath, The Fear gorged itself. Steaming offal bathed The Fear with its aroma. It was a distinctly sexual feeling, an aphrodisiac, spread like a garnish, though The Fear knew nothing of this. To it, feeding was fucking.

Its jaws clamped over the thing's sex organs, spread out before it so invitingly. It was then that the thing's screams petered out and dwindled to an unconscious moan, of pleasure or delirium or that song a creature sings on its way into death, The Fear did not know.

Finally, after a sex-caressing eternity, The Fear detached itself.

The Cardigan Man was nothing more than a few scraps of splintered bone, sucked of their marrow and dry of any trace of lifeblood.

The Fear continued through the tunnel, pushing past ribs of fabric, and emerged from the cocoon into the bathroom. It saw its reflection in the mirror, saw what it had become, and a strange feeling came over it. It screamed at what it saw. Its claw darted forward like a piston and slammed the mirror into spiderwebbed shards of silver.

Jack was gone.

She was The Fear now.

IT EMERGED TO BLAZING GUNFIRE. Its flowers darted inside its carapace; teeth zippered shut with an audible *zzzclick*. Plates knitted together across its body and bullets pinged off it, ricocheting around the apartment. It had gorged itself in the closet, yes, but still it hungered; it was so impossibly *hungry*, insatiable, a thirst that would never be quenched until the world was drained of blood. The men streamed into the apartment, lining themselves up as a veritable feast, and The Fear accepted their offering with a roar. Bullets whizzed, sang through the air, and its flowers sang in harmony, humming safely behind plated armor. It ripped an assault rifle from the hands of one of the men and used it to wipe his scraggly, white-powdered beard from his face in a spurt of blood. It tossed the weapon and descended upon the man, and he screamed as it fed upon him. Its flowers peeked their throats out to dip themselves into his veins and soak themselves in drink. It ripped his arms from his body with a *pop* and *crunch* and his sockets were fountains of Merlot. Then another man, falling beneath its claws, and another, and another.

The Fear grew.

It felt its back pop, scales expanding, new seams erupting like tributaries of a river across its back, seams of teeth and flowers and . . . *something else* . . . *something new* . . .

"What the fuck," a man shouted. *"WHAT THE FUCK?!"*

Guns blazed. Men screamed.

The Fear grew.

Leathery tugs and rips snapped across its back as the new seams spread wide to give egress to the new folds of . . . *something* . . . vast and terrible to behold.

Wings, two great big bat-like wings, erupted from its shoulder blades, unfolding and fanning out and catching scatters of bullets that fell pinging to the carpet like dropped quarters.

The Fear stretched its new appendages, shrieking in revelatory lust, purring like an engine. It batted away the last few intruders like tin soldiers. It leapt, bounding over the husks of the men it had devoured.

The window.

Broken and gaping wide.

Freeeeeeeeeeedom . . .

In one bounding leap it soared out of the large,

shattered frame of the window, spreading its great flapping wings. Warm pockets of air *whooshed* beneath its wings as it pumped them down and sent itself climbing in the humid, storm-quenched air.

It flew from its old life.

The Fear spread its wings and soared.

Join my newsletter for a FREE copy of my upcoming exclusive novel, *Welcome to SmileyLand*, and to stay up to date on all future monstrous projects.

www.SpencerHamiltonBooks.com

Please review!

Reviews are the best way for other readers to find books they enjoy. A few minutes of your time to leave a review of *The Fear* at your preferred retailer would be greatly appreciated.

Thank you for reading!

ACKNOWLEDGMENTS

And I thought writing *Kitchen Sink* was hard.

The Fear isn't the first novel I've written, but it is the first novel I've completed, which I now know takes a lot more than just an imagination and a word processor. What follows is a list of all the people who were indispensable in this book's creation:

Amy Teegan, my editor, who had her hand in every step of this process and is a certifiable genius. Landon Borup, my boss and slave driver and brother and constant support. David Burchell, my above-and-beyond beta reader. Cecilia Şenocak, my sensitivity reader. Jamie Davis, my medical fact-checker (if I still managed to screw it up, blame me, not him). Milan Jovanovic, whose brilliant cover design informed so much of this novel. Sandeep Likhar, for another beautiful interior design. Nick Harper, whose eagerness to illustrate that final transformation of The Fear helped me push through to the end. Natalie Naudus, whose audiobook narration brings Ash and Jack to life in a way my words alone never could.

And, finally, to you, the reader. I cannot thank you enough for giving this book your time and energy.

Much of this novel was inspired by my own life, and

to that end, if I have done my job as the author and Jack and Ash's story felt real to you, I'd like to take a moment to address the mental health issues which my characters were not fully equipped to handle. If you or someone you love is struggling, please do not hesitate to seek help.

One last thing, to anyone who needs to hear it:

Don't panic. It's not the end of the world.

Spencer Hamilton
August 2020

ABOUT THE AUTHOR

Spencer Hamilton lives in Austin, Texas. His first book, *Kitchen Sink*, is a short story collection. *The Fear* is his first novel.